I0610956

Catharsis

Rafael Samuel García-Cortés

Catharsis

First Edition: 2023

ISBN: 9781524318383
ISBN eBook: 9781524328351

© of the text:
   Rafael Samuel García-Cortés

© Layout, design and production of this edition: 2023 EBL

To my dear Camila, Sofía and Alison:
I will love you forever.

Table of Contents

∫∫First

In that moment, lying in a fetal position, Sebastián witnessed the first omen of the end of his life. The dream was so vivid that he could even perceive the annoying medals he wore over his military uniform. There, only inches away from glory, he felt imprisoned by the orchid perfume swaying between his arms.

Without a doubt, his dancing partner was beautiful. From a distance one could observe how the soldier enjoyed each atom of her existence. It was almost impossible not to fall prey to her gaze and flirtatious smile. That evening, she was wearing a long black dress that brushed her body from her shoulders, all the way down to her ankles. At some point, between the steps and turns of their slow dance, the young man felt the peculiar certainty that he was daydreaming.

Without knowing why, every second of that evening seemed important, somewhat special. The music kept playing in the distance, the ballroom and the dance floor kept spinning, while his body felt the incipient symptoms of love invading a lonely heart. Everything around him was happening almost in slow motion, to the beat of an old, simple ballad. In such a way the evening went by, until he felt the advent of a bad premonition.

First, a slight shiver over his spine turned into uneasiness and, suddenly, that sea of joy in which he had been bathing, while he was dancing, began to evaporate and dehydrate, becoming arid and thick, until it ended up crumbling like a sandcastle of sadness on a depressive and lonely beach. The ground stopped its spinning and became opaque. The music followed suit, as it became disfigured and turned into the deafening memories of war nestled within his consciousness. Then, an infinite sea of guilt grew and expanded, until it dug deep within the confines of his being, serving as the point of origin for a rhythm of anguish that devastated every inch of his soul and ablated every space in his memory.

The man felt fear. He naively wanted to take refuge in the gaze of the woman he held in his arms, but it was impossible: she, the one from a few moments ago, was no longer the same. That beautiful lady seemed to have aged in a matter of minutes. As he looked at her, he realized that his young dancing partner had been withered by more than fifty years of wrinkles. Right after seeing the ravages of time upon her, he had the odd certainty that this woman meant more than just a date, for the person he studied so closely appeared to be his wife. "But how can she be my wife if I am not yet married?" the incredulous sleeper silently asked himself. After several moments of cognitive struggle, having run through every second of his momentary reality in excruciating detail, the man realized that in reality he was not that forlorn military man with devastating war memories. During that evening filled with elusive dreams, he had simply been given the task of inhabiting the troubled mind of a human being torn apart by his past.

Slowly, deep within his dreams, he struggled within himself, until he managed to come back from the depressive trance caused by that revealing vision. It was then that he was finally convinced that he was not that military man dancing on the dance floor next to an aging lady. "How real this feels!", he thought, immersed in his dreams, without realizing that, at that very moment, in that apparently innocent siesta, Sebastián was experiencing firsthand the military memories that belonged to his father, Sgt. Samuel Luis Pérez.

As soon as he opened his eyes, Sebastián was repeatedly thankful that he had been sleeping. He was lying on his bed, covered in sweat from head to toe. He was thirsty; his throat was dry. "Did I snore?" he thought, as he swallowed a thick gulp of useless saliva.

In his bedroom there were several portraits hanging on the wall. The pictures showed versions of himself at different ages. There were photographs of him with his brother playing as kids at the lake house; of his entire family having dinner as adults. Despite the passage of time across the photos it was obviously Sebastián in all of them. In the pictures you could see his large face and long, pointed, exuberant nose. On his right cheek he had a small but noticeable mole that, depending on the quality of the razor, could be seen or missed. His eyes were disproportionately large (almost as if inherited from a *coquí* frog) with a dark brown color that bordered on the black of his hair. In short: Sebastián was a tall, very pale, middle-aged, Puerto Rican man with very large, almost black eyes and an exaggerated nose.

The air was heavy. He noticed after awakening and realized that it was well past lunchtime; his siesta had lasted far longer than he'd imagined. The sky was lowering, its clouds varying between a dark gray bordering on purple and a deep black that spread everywhere. Sebastián appeared to be in no hurry. Slowly, he glanced at his wristwatch and noticed that it read 10:23 p.m. with 30, 31, 32... seconds. Then he closed his eyes and pretended he wasn't trying to calculate that it had already been approximately 11 hours and 30, 31, 32... seconds since he had left his doctor's office to go to lunch. In reality, he was not affected by having overslept during a day's work. In fact, for the past three months, he had opened his clinic for an average of four hours, three times a week.

Throughout medical circles, there were more than enough rumors about Dr. Sebastián Luis Pérez-Fuertes and how unwell he was looking lately. Sebastián, in general, was not affected by gossiping. That being said, over the past few months the rumors continued to grow exponentially and with good reason. "Even if he graduated with honors, he's a lousy physician," his past patients would say behind his back. "I heard his mother forced him to be a doctor," said others. Deep down, he knew that those people were not gossipmongers, but hypocrites, since everything they said was true, even though they never confronted him face to face. Certainly, people were not lying when they proclaimed that, at that time in his life, he was terrible at taking care of his patients and, moreover, that he was almost forced by his mother to enroll in medical school. During those days, Dr. Sebastián Pérez-Fuertes was probably the worst version of a physician imaginable.

Seba, as he was nicknamed outside the office, used to shower as soon as he woke up. His rinse after that long sleep was quick and in less than a couple of minutes he managed to shake the rest of the sleep from his eyes, along with the memories of his father dancing with his mother. Once dressed, he turned on his cell phone, grabbed his keys, his wallet and started to head out of his apartment which was in the outskirts of Old San Juan. However, just before leaving his room, he noticed that on his nightstand lay a note written in black India ink. Intrigued, he walked towards it and, picking it up, read it in amazement:

You have one year to live

A few milliseconds after reading the note, Sebastián's heart felt the impact of an adrenergic shock originating deep within his gut, followed by a cocktail of epinephrine, serotonin and a couple of drops of dopamine, which mixed quite well to take over his brain and each one of his neurons, until his chest was pounding at a rate of 184 beats per minute. With every heartbeat, his senses expanded each one of his major veins and arteries, steering him, without escape, to the confines of his worst nightmares, those in which he was loved by no one and died like a bum, lying alone, empty and hopeless on the ground.

As soon as his pupils were dilated and each one of his muscles were pre-excited, his brain demanded that his eyes looked everywhere, as his aura, in desperation, rose, once and for all, to the top of the ceiling. From there, he realized that he was no longer framed within his body but was now separated from his anatomy and the rest of his soul. He then began the search for the person who had dared to announce his death. With no idea who it might be, he began by combing under his bed and over the sink, up through the cabinets, inspecting every plate, cooking utensil, wine glass, and piece of trash found in his kitchen.

He certainly felt light, like a gas that floated along every edge of his sad existence, crossing the living room and each piece of his furniture, passing over the carpet, until he stopped frantically on his living room table. There he looked and found nothing but several ants along a lonely and completely dry beer can. Then he moved quickly to his cell phone, which he used to be transported to some happier place near the center of Paris, where he wandered through the streets, bathed in yellow lights and discreet cafes, strolling among Rodin's sculptures and admiring a couple of thousand works signed by Picasso. Aimlessly, he decided to run through the *Tuileries* gardens and, tired of loitering pointlessly, he converted his being into a lost tourist, using his cell phone to arrive back in his bedroom, via his computer monitor.

Once back in his apartment, in Old San Juan, Puerto Rico, he wandered through the Melquíades parchments, which he adored so much, reviewed a couple of Neruda poems and browsed through the hundred or so dusty medical books he owned, until, bored with prowling around like a psychotic spirit, he realized that, perhaps, the healthiest thing to do was to return to his body.

Once he regained his senses, he found himself enclosed by his skin and framed by that infinite sadness which defined him. At that moment he understood that it was probably ridiculous to try to find the author who had warned him of something impossible. If he was going to die of anything in this life, it would surely be the painful habit of putting up with his mother, Doña Mother.

∫∫Second

As he left his apartment, Seba regretted not having put on a sports jacket. The weather was chilly and, for that reason, he decided to put his hands inside his front pockets, which still held an old pack of gum, his keys and his cell phone. After the rampage produced by the note, Sebastián tried to convince himself that perhaps it had been a bad joke planned by his brother and, because he did not want to give him the satisfaction of seeing him frightened, he preferred to relax and pretend that it had never happened. He then passed one, two, three and, at the fourth car, he decided to venture out and cross the avenue. Once he stood on the opposite sidewalk, he stopped and felt his fingers trembling inside his left pocket.

"Hello," answered Seba.

"Where are you?" asked Doña Mother, his mother.

He wasn't surprised to not hear a "How are you, my dear son? Let alone a, "Hello, my darling!", so everything was definitely going very well in his mother's house.

"I'm out and I'm busy. Do you need anything?" asked Seba.

"No," replied his mother, "I just wanted to hear the beautiful voice of my favorite son."

In truth, Seba knew his mother had no favorite children. She said the same to both Seba and Ian. One thing was certain though, she wanted to hear her younger son's voice that night. After a pause, Doña Mother continued with her questions:

"Where have you been? What have you been doing? Who are you with? Some woman? You sound hoarse, have you been smoking?"

After hearing these words, Sebastián felt as if a strike of fury took over his throat, attempting to turn the color of his eyes from dark brown to red, as his right hand was about to crush his mobile phone into pieces. So, in order not to fork out a few hundred dollars for a new cell phone, or to permanently discolor his eyes , he decided to cut the call. Actually, it was not a major problem, he was already accustomed to the escape-protocol he'd designed with his brother to deal with their mother. Once Doña Mother began one of her peculiar performances, the ritual was impeccably executed to avoid further consequences. This was a perfect occasion not to get angry; the night was exquisite and there was no reason to waste it in anger.

Once he calmed down, he continued walking until he turned right at the corner of Steffani and Luchetti, stopping at *El Bar del Murciégalo.*

This bar, whose name literally translates to something like, "The Flittermouse's Bar" in old English, was an absolute dive. Everything about it, from its name to the facade, was a fiasco. The paint on the walls was dismal and the smell seemed to come from each of the 6.022×10^{23} particles per mole of guano that surrounded the decrepit building. Curiously, the place could have been named by any drunkard who knew the two wingless bats that inhabited it. "*The twuo ratzzz arre my budddiesz,*" Sebastián kept repeating with a slur after the tenth beer. "*I even named them and adopted them. The vite one I call her Hiswife and the darkel one is Hislover. I curze the mother whoeber deh-darez to screuw wit' them.*" From time to time, he would be heard making jokes with them, he would say things like, "*Bohth of jou com' wit' me. Guyzsz, if anyone, anyyyy-one, comez looking for mei, tell 'em that I left vith Hiswife and Hislover"*. However, as they were inside jokes, no one laughed or really cared.

The walls of that bar looked as if they were sweating; they were dark and from them hung pieces of black paint with signs of moisture and a parched, grayish fungus. He usually sat in a corner of the bar that normally would hold six or seven people. On the other side of the table, almost always, sat Antonio. He was a man in his 60s, who paced, coughed and spoke with such deep hoarseness that he sounded closer to 80 years of age. On the ceiling was an electric fan that spun with a very faint, rhythmic screech. Despite the shambles and even though Sebastián had enough money to drink champagne in any fancy social club, he always preferred that little bar, because he felt that no one recognized him there and its decadent facade bordered between the unique and the original. In essence, the anonymity and mediocrity of *El Bar del Murciégalo* made him feel special.

It was 11:53 p.m. when Seba felt his left thigh vibrate again, so he decided to answer his cell phone.

"Hello, Do-ña Mo-ther," said Seba, slightly worse for wear after seventy-five fluid ounces or 6.25 bottles of beer.

"Mother? May God and all his saints save me from being anything like your mother. Do you know what time it is, you irresponsible little drunk?" asked a woman in an agitated manner.

Without a doubt, it was the unmistakable voice of Natalia, who was his clinic manager/personal fixer/counselor/previous lover/now almost platonic sister. She was the sole reason why the train of his life had not derailed and overturned in one of the million turns it had taken since he had known her.

"It izsz, humm, it is, like, about eleven o'clock, isn't it?" he answered.

Natalia remained silent for several seconds. Once this lapse was over, she let out each and every one of the vowels, verbs, prepositions, phrases and sentences that made up the totality of insults that crossed her mind.

"No, it izsz not like eleven o'clock. It's fifty-three minutes and thirty-three seconds past eleven, but how could you be expected to know that when I can smell the stench of who knows how many beers you must have had? Instead of calling me and asking what the hell I did to get rid of the twenty-three patients with appointments that you stood up in the office when you said you were going to lunch and would be right back. I imagine you also didn't notice the 253 calls or text messages I left on your cell phone trying to figure out where the hell you were. No, no, no, no, you couldn't possibly tell me your plans, that would be way too difficult, too gentlemanly, professional, or, perhaps, polite. What else can you expect if working three days a week is too tormenting for his majesty? Why not work two and a half days and forget about the whole world? Anyway, I know you don't care about anything, you already have money, luxuries, your qualifications, but I'm fed up; tired of continuing with this game. This time you've gone too far and don't think you're going to get away with it."

Sebastián chose each of the one hundred words he said and spoke them with such effort that it would have taken a blood alcohol test to know that he had, indeed, ingested alcoholic beverages. The delicacy was because he knew how fragile the line was between Natalia forgiving him or becoming his *ex-everything*.

"Natalia," he said in a very subtle and cautious tone, "I swear it was not my intention to hurt anyone, especially you: forgive me. What happened was that, after eating lunch, I felt sick to my stomach. I had colicky gas and I went home to use the bathroom. There I found myself quite unwell and decided to take two doses of that medicine that I usually prescribe to you when you are sick, but as you know it contains opioids, a drug that, besides being therapeutic against diarrhea, causes an inhibitory effect in the central nervous system. So, as a consequence, it made me drowsy and I inadvertently fell asleep."

She really didn't know anything about pharmacology. And, even if she did know a little, Dr. Pérez-Fuertes had just made a plausible mix between his fictitious diarrhea and a real drug. Cleverly, Sebastián had chosen to attack Natalia's ego, in order to support an argument that every single person who knew him was aware to be false. On the other end of the phone, Natalia paused again for a couple of seconds and decided not to hang up, so as to answer the apology.

"I don't care. You, more than anyone else, a doctor by profession, trained for almost ten years in gastroenterology, should have known better than to give yourself two doses of that devilish drug in the middle of a clinic day. Now you're in trouble and you're going to have to come up with a better excuse to explain yourself to the insurers."

The physician was silent for a moment.

"What does it matter to them what happened?" he asked.

"They care. And a lot. Since a sixty-eight or sixty-nine-year-old woman had to be taken to the ER while she was stood in *your* office waiting room, because *you* were not on time for her post-procedure medical appointment after having a colonoscopy done the day prior, which *you* yourself suggested, ordered, finalized and which *you* alone signed. *You* advised her that if she developed any kind of bleeding, complications or if she developed any kind of discomfort, she needed to come to the clinic or go to the hospital. Well, imagine what happened, she came in with abdominal pain and rectal bleeding, but after spending six hours in our waiting room she ended up passing out, collapsing to the floor and we had to call an ambulance. God willing, she is still alive, but her vitals were dismal and I even heard the paramedics giving her chest compressions in the ambulance before rushing her to the ER. I already called the insurers and the medical liability lawyers, because that was what we agreed after the four lawsuits last year and they want to have all the facts up to date, along with the lady's medical records, just in case one of the family members "is not blind" and promptly proceeds to sue you," Natalia replied sarcastically.

"Well, I'll have to go and talk to the legal team early during the next week. I have to take a couple of days off. But just so you know, if the lady died in connection with the procedure, it was not through lack of skill on my part; it was the fault of the emergency medical system. Moreover, I am a doctor, not Jesus Christ, so even if I had given her a post-procedure rectal bleed, if she was not properly prepared, with clean bowels, for a colonoscopy, I would have done the same thing and called an ambulance. So, I don't think it would have changed her outcome," said Sebastián, a little defiant.

"No, don't worry, your *highness* is never guilty of anything. What you forget is that you don't have to fire a gun to be a thug. Sometimes, not helping to save someone is equivalent to pulling a trigger." There was a click and the call died.

Natalia was a quiet lady, quite polite, well dressed and classy. Her light blue eyes and tender gaze were very difficult to forget. Her hair was mostly straight and brown, with light and innocuous curls that rested on her shoulders. She still retained the traces of a shy smile, worn down by the bad times gifted by her boss, who was almost like a thirty-seven-year-old child to her. Her skin was very soft; in fact, for many years, it was this last detail that Sebastián missed the most when he thought of her. He would also remember her smell, the texture of her lips and, above all, her unconditional love for him. Together they shared six years as sweethearts and, during this period, there were many smiles, but also many tears. They began dating the same year that Sebastián graduated from medical school while he was completing his residency at the Puerto Rico Medical Center. Then, they continued their courtship after he obtained his subspecialty and together, they established his Gastroenterology Medical Office. Thus, they had an adult relationship until, one awful day, Natalia asked him if he ever saw a future in which they were married, creating a family and raising children of their own. He was honest with her and told her no, that he hated the idea of having a family and never wanted children. He tried to tell her that, irrespective of this, he loved her very much and that he wanted to stay with her, to be sweethearts. Initially, Natalia did not know how to react to his reply so she simply cried. She cried so much during that night that the hours on the clock were flooded by her sadness and she slowly found herself floating for long hours on that sea of tears that Sebastián had caused. When she woke up, she realized that her love had turned to nostalgia and decided to end their relationship without any fight. On her part there was no shouting, no reproaches, but rather, Natalia simply kept quiet and pretended to have instantly forgiven him. Although Sebastián initially did not want to marry her, it took him more than a year to come to terms with the idea that he had lost her forever as a life partner. Deep inside, he always hoped she would be there, waiting for him to change his mind. It wasn't until Natalia got engaged to her now husband that Seba decided to forget her completely and accept seeing her as a sister, just as she had, since the day they ended their relationship, seen him as a brother.

Even though they had ended their engagement, Natalia decided to continue working as his manager and administrative assistant for the simple fact that he paid her too well and, in reality, she did not feel any resentment. And he allowed her to keep her job because he knew that otherwise his life would become a complete waste. So, the two of them had continued a relationship of pure friendship, for five years now, which they both knew was not perfect, but which they also both needed. However, above and beyond that supposedly simulated fraternal love and their withered romance, they always knew that there was a good chemistry between them.

Sebastián had just finished talking to Natalia on his cell phone and he felt his ears flush with anger. With the sad excuse of waiting for his temper to subside, he decided to stay a bit longer and resume his drunken sojourn again. He joked for a while with *Hiswife* and *Hislover*, chatted a bit with Toño, the drunkard in the corner, who for some reason was sober that night and, at about 8.75 beers after having hung up, he ordered another cold beer from Antonio, "to go", and started his way back to his apartment. For this he walked to the left for two and a half sips of his drink. As soon as he reached the intersection with Steffani Street, he turned left again, walked about three more sips and waited for one, two and three burps to flow from his esophagus before crossing the deserted street. Painstakingly, but with great technique, he climbed the seventeen steps to his apartment. Once inside, he made sure to lock and bolt the door, drank four glasses of water and lay back on his pillow. When he closed his eyes, almost 15.75 beers had passed since he received the threatening note, although at that moment it didn't matter, the alcohol had already taken control of his nervous system and that omen, in his mind, had been relegated to just a misunderstanding.

∫∫Third

Sebastián had a very small nuclear family. It basically consisted of his mother, father and an older brother. His mom, Doña Mother, had acquired as an adult the habit of never, ever, being called by her birth name: Dolores Fuertes. Such was her urgency to change her name that as soon as she got married, she displaced her last name and threw it as far away as she could. As the years went by, she was known as Dolores Pérez, until later she did the same with the rest of her name. Now, her name was simply, Doña Mother. "I gave birth to two very fat children, that's all," she repeated to herself when it came to annihilating the complexes that were born on her reflection. "I'm not fat, I'm just full of love," she repeated from time to time when chatting with the girls in the beauty salon. Truthfully, that bitter, unfriendly, wrinkled and fattened image she carried these days hid a very young, sweet and delicate version of herself that once made her, and everyone for that matter, happier. Now, the years had hidden her youth, shrunk her happiness, shattered her delicate figure and tarnished her charisma. It was as if a perfect lady had been swallowed by a life preserver full of misery and subcutaneous bitterness, which made her look significantly obese.

Sebastián had a brother, two years older, named Ian. Two strangers walking on the street share approximately 99.9% of their DNA. For full siblings, this number rises to 99.95%. Despite sharing all of this genetic similarity, the truth is that there was much more than 0.05% difference between them. You may be wondering, "How big of a difference can 0.05% be?". Quite a bit. But let's start with the similarities: they were both tall, Puerto Rican and light-skinned. That was it. In contrast, Ian was a civil engineer and not a medical doctor, he had freckles on his cheeks that were almost the same brown as his hair, he loved his job regardless of his salary, was especially attentive to his clients and tolerated his family infinitely more than his younger, doctor brother. Additionally, Ian graduated at the age of twenty-three and decided that same year to open his own engineering firm. Sebastián, on the other hand, took much longer to become a true professional at what he did. Firstly, because a degree in medicine takes somewhat longer than one in engineering. But, secondly, because although Seba received his diploma in gastroenterology at the age of thirty-one, it was not until he was thirty-seven years old that he learned to love his job.

In terms of personality, it can be said that the two were polar opposites. This was observed very early in their childhood. Ian will never forget the day when, at the age of nine, he had an unbridled fight with Sebastián. That day was the birthday of his father, Sgt. Samuel L. Pérez and, as punishment for the riot, he locked them both in their respective rooms so that, as he would say, "They could blow off some steam hitting the walls." Without knowing it, that immature brawl with his younger brother would end up being one of the biggest reasons why their personalities would take opposite directions.

Ian was not uncomfortable talking to the walls. In fact, with the simple purpose of annoying his father, he would shout out the numbers from one to one hundred for hours on end until exhaustion got the better of him. On that occasion he began with the same tenacious motivation of trying to prove that he hated the system and that he would not follow it. "... twenty-eight, twenty-nine, thirty...", the boy shouted, when suddenly he heard that phrase he would never forget: "Could you keep your voice down?"

Ian was left dry, paralyzed and in suspense. "... thirty-one, thirty-two, thirty-three...", he tried to count again, but, before he vocalized that divine age figure, he heard the same voice repeat in a more articulate tone, "Please, could you lower your voice?" Ian stood up and, in one and a half turns, landed with the occipital part of his skull buried on the wall. In that instant, he felt terrified and short of breath, utterly frail and mute. He tried to speak, but nothing happened. He tried to get up, but not one of his six hundred striated muscles decided to respond. Desperately, he wanted to visualize the author of those words. As he turned his neck, he suffered chills, fever, general malaise, urinary incontinence and even nausea. At nine years old, he felt as if he was condemned to death.

But where did this voice come from? Well, in front of Ian was a small decorative night lamp that seemed to be able to speak and communicate with him.

"What did you say?" asked Ian.

"Please, could you keep your voice down?" Ernie replied.

Ernie was quite normal. Just as normal as a unicorn or a fairy tale. He was approximately two and a half foot tall and eight inches wide. In essence, he was just an infant's lamp that morphologically imitated an elf dressed in green but was able to talk. Its image was funny and childish, not at all frightening.

"You... you can talk?" asked Ian, almost in tears.

"Yes, Mr. Ian, I can talk, think, advise and even cry if you need me," replied the little elf.

"You promise to be my friend and not hurt me?" Ian muttered.

"Yes, of course I will, I promise to be your best friend, forever," Ernie replied.

In reality, Ernie was just a lamp to everyone except Ian; his voice could not be heard by any other mortal ear. Many times, during their childhood, they heard Ian talking to himself and, upon entering his bedroom, they would simply find him standing by his small, well-lit friend. To the world, Ernie was as sessile as a Michelangelo sculpture and as expressive as a rock. If you ask any psychiatrist, they will tell you that it was a hallucination created by Ian, provoked by a state of psychosis, as he screamed in anguish during that day. But science cannot always explain the exact reason for the birth of a friendship, whether it is imaginary or not. From then on, the only truth that matter was that this illuminated elf figurine became his best friend. That day full of fights with his brother, a spoiled birthday party for his father and a burst of anger against his bedroom walls would serve as the genesis for a symbiotic relationship that would last until the last day of their lives.

∫∫Fourth

It entered slowly, through the only corner of the curtains it could. Once inside the bedroom, the sad little ray of sunlight guided its wave-particle skeleton across the room until it reached Ian's left eye. Along with its heat, it brought with it nearly eight light-minutes of delay since it fled from the sun.

"Damn sun," Ernie muttered.

"Shhhh, I want to sleep," said Ian with the bedsheets rolled up between his teeth and his stomach.

Even though it was Friday and he had to get up early for work, it was not uncommon to find Ian in his bed until after noon. He was tired but decided to turn off his digital alarm as a message reading "*Good morning*" was projected onto his ceiling. "*Good morning*," Ian thought as he coughed, "what does this clock know of the difference between good and bad days?" Ernie, on the other hand, "*Good morning*" or not, loved the image of the little red light shining over the room from the digital alarm, as it made him feel more human.

After turning off the alarm, Ian grabbed his slippers and looked at Ernie.

"Yes, I know, I'll close the curtains."

"Thank you," said the elf and returned to his usual motionless pose.

Next, he decided to take a shower in an attempt to shake his tiredness. Once he turned on the sprinkler head, the first thing he saw was a drop, followed by hundreds of thousands (practically countless) more. On his face was the full weight of a warm, refreshing wave. For an instant, that fountain of water made him happy.

"There was a water trickle in the shower," he sang to himself, as he remembered an old Spanish nursery rhyme, "*La Fuente del Chorrito*", and he let out a disbelieving laugh. Unbeknownst to him, his observation awakened the restlessness of something within that group of droplets and, quietly and introvertedly, a trickle separated from the hundred thousand around him. That trickle grew angrily as Ian continued to sing in Spanish, "it got big" and "it got little."

"Why are you in a bad mood?" asked Ian as he laughed. "Let me guess, poor squirt, are you hot?"

But his laughter did not please Mr. Squirt and he became unbalanced. Suddenly, and as heated as he was, the water jet separated himself from the mass and, in a precise and premeditated way, whipped each of his hydrogen bonds across Ian's cheeks. The slap was so hard that he fell on his butt and each of his teeth throbbed above and below his gums. Instead of getting up, turning off the shower and running out to dry off, Ian decided to try to get even.

"Go to hell" he shouted, followed by something along the lines of, "I'll never let myself be screwed by a stupid little handful of someone's imaginary water." It almost sounded like a declaration of war on a measly, non-sentient, water battalion.

The reality was that Ian was outnumbered even before he began to irrationally stomp on the droplets of water that appeared before his eyes. As a result of his shouting and stomping, he managed to enrage the remaining 3,592 jets of aquatic bonds that were present. In the shower there were squirters of all kinds: baby squirters, giant squirters, a trapeze artist, a couple of rainy ones, dancers, poets, painters and even a fisherman or two. As soon as Ian realized the severity of his actions, he tried to run away and get out of the shower, but it was too late, all the jets were furious. Instantly, they were flying everywhere. In fact, every water source in his bathroom opened up and it seemed as if a huge gang of people were ready to put him in his place. Right off the bat, every molecule of H_2O began to beat him down, retaliating with every fist for his stupid questions. Most of the bruises came from the shower, though the most painful spurts were from the sink, bidet and toilet, as they came from unexpected sources. In unison, those wet clusters assaulted every one of the twenty-one square feet of his skin. In his desperation to protect himself, Ian managed to cushion a few of them by wrapping himself in the shower curtain, but he still had to suffer the full brunt of that never-before seen or experienced fury.

Lying on the ground, he felt as though every part of his body had been run over that morning. The impacts were such that, as he blinked, he felt pain just below his eyelashes. As he breathed, he whispered in agony on both sides of his ribs and whenever he accidentally touched his abdomen, he felt tears welling up. In general, all the lashes were precise and delivered with such rage that Ian thought he would never get out of that bathroom alive.

"I'm sorry," he said as he began to cry. "I'm so sorry, Mr. Squirt," he repeated as he coughed and spat full mouthfuls of blood onto the floor. In total, from start to finish, that sweep lasted approximately one hundred and twenty-three seconds and it wasn't until he apologized to all of Mr. Squirt's relatives that he managed to make it out of the bathroom. Once outside, he lay face up on the floor of his bedroom.

"What the hell happened to you?" Ernie called when he saw him on the ground.

"I was beaten up by more than a thousand jets of water and I can't even breathe. Damn them all, even if they do make up seventy-one percent of the planet!" he replied.

Ian Samuel was naked from head to toe. As he gathered the strength to get up, Ernie saw every lashing on his best friend's body. On his skin hung the bruises which had tattooed it in varying shades of purple and brown. On his right buttock he had a wine-colored one with small, very dark spots all around. On the right side of his chest, he had an empty space, resembling what one would imagine to be the result of a run-in with a padded door. Lastly, Ian displayed a small cut over his lower lip that also showed signs of requiring a pair of stitches.

"Ian, go on, call your brother and tell him what happened to you, he'll surely give you a hand," said Ernie though the reality was that his best friend was already sore enough to ignore the advice.

This time the elf was right: he needed the help of his doctor brother, Sebastián. In pain, he crawled as best he could to call Seba, but as soon as he began to dial the number, he felt that recurring scent that identified Dalymar Lávi.

Sebastián was driving when he received a call from his brother in his car.

"Hi, bro!" Sebastián answered in a falsely cheerful tone.

By that time, exactly seven days had passed since the incident of the first mysterious note. At that precise moment, Seba was returning from an appointment with his insurer and his cheerful tone was nothing more than theater. As he answered the call, he was driving his car. "Second gear, no-clutch; third, speed up, fourth, no-clutch; third, lady, old man, slow down, that was close, no-clutch," was all that his mind whispered to him.

"I need help, brother. I just blew a gasket in the bathtub and I want you to examine me so you can tell me if I need to go to the ER today or not," stammered Ian through sore teeth.

"What? Are you crazy? Why go to the ER? For a second opinion? Ian, I'm 'the-family-doctor' and don't worry, you'll be as good as new. Give me twenty minutes and I'll come to your apartment, I am actively typing your address in my GPS, we'll talk in a moment." A click was heard as they both hung up.

Lying on the floor, approximately seventeen minutes before Seba arrived, Ian went through the motions of putting on boxers and shorts. Leaning on his side, he again remembered Dalymar, the love of his life, the girl with red curls who starred in his days from the age of twelve to the present. He still remembered the date she died. How could he forget that day when his love for life died with her?

Physically, Dalymar Laví died on a dark morning of a November first, after having received her morning pulmonary therapy. Everyone was devastated. Partly out of grief and partly because she had been, for twenty-two years the princess of the Pérez-Fuertes family, their adoptive daughter and sister. For them, she was the most beautiful flower that no one was allowed to touch or harm. Ever since she and Ian fell in love, his family cared for her like one of their own. After Daly's (as she was affectionately called) death, Ian Samuel developed a severe bout of depression, which almost drove him to suicide. First, he stopped eating and bathing. Then, he slowly stopped talking to his friends, followed by his family and, as the days went by, he withdrew completely into his own world until he became practically a hermit, living in his garbage-strewn apartment. During those days, he became so mentally ill that for long periods of time he forgot he was alive. The family tried just about everything: psychologists, psychiatrists, some more realistic medications and even alternative treatments, they submitted him to electroshock therapies, hired graduate nurses to watch him every second and a maid to attend to him around the clock. It wasn't until a year after her death that he miraculously began to improve. In less than a week he began to converse and to eat more than the minimum necessary to subsist. Gradually the doctors began to see tangible improvements and after two months of absolute progress he even stopped taking the antidepressant medications. Incredibly, in less than three months, he went from being bedridden to walking with the help of physiotherapy and feeding himself. Three months later (almost six months since he began to improve) he was ready to face the world again; something no one ever imagined would happen again. Ian had miraculously managed to find the perfect remedy for his recovery without his family and medical specialists.

"Are you feeling better?" asked Dalymar, twelve minutes before Sebastián arrived.

"Not really, but Seba is on his way, so don't worry," Ian replied.

Like a cyclical mirage, Daly would appear and vanish, quite regularly, to talk to him, to say hello and hug him, or just to be with him. That was precisely the prescription that had managed to cure him from that suicidal depression that almost led to his death. For Ian, the image of Dalymar was real, tangible and identical to that of the sweet woman who died alone in a hospital bed in San Juan. Her neck was still intact, very long and slender. Her hands were the same, as delicate as the texture of her lips, and her left hand still bore her wedding ring, which made them so happy on a daily basis. Her scent was still unmistakable, despite her death and the years between; many times, her perfume was perceptible to everyone around her, especially Ian's father, Don Samy, and the rest of her family. Truly, Daly's fragrance never left Ian's life and her scent was seductive, yet tender, and its only purpose was to remind Ian how much she loved him. For him, fragrance or not, certainly having her present and remaining by his side was a heavenly garden. So, even though Dalymar had died, he was still lucky enough to see her (real or not) in his world on a daily basis, so that he could hold her, talk to her and even make love to her. This is why Ian Samuel always worked from his apartment and hated going outside if it wasn't absolutely necessary.

Seven minutes before Seba arrived, Ian decided to get up from the floor and lie down next to Daly.

"I love you, Daly, I love you so much," said Ian as he lay down on his bed.

As soon as he touched the sheets, he felt a great desire to stretch out her arms and embrace that angel lying next to him. Around him, he felt each one of his bruises slowly go to sleep and at the same time he began to feel a deep throbbing coming from his upper thighs. With every second, the throbbing grew and grew progressively stronger with the certainty of his partner's unique perfume. Just after he embraced her, he received a kiss from Daly behind his ear, while she placed a sheet over Ernie to hide the scene. Gradually, their hips came together and Daly placed her legs around him, so she could continue to feel the rhythmic throbbing between his thighs. Five minutes before his brother arrived, Ian slid his fingers down Daly's body and with a subtle caress removed the cuffs of her blouse as he placed her in some corner of their mutual fantasy. The kisses grew faster and deeper just four minutes and twenty-three seconds before Seba arrived. Dalymar's pink breasts were unrestrained as she moved in front of Ian, who appeared to be spellbound by her. There, three minutes and fifty-three seconds before Seba knocked on the front door, he removed, gently, the bottom of Dalymar's underwear and slowly slipped his body inside her. Slowly at first and every second a little faster, their bodies merged into one, forming a mixture of lust in which they both swayed to the same wet, addictive drumbeat that choreographed their sexuality. A low moan from Dalymar, followed by a discreet cry and a small nibble, were all he needed to drive him mad with desire. Inside her, Ian felt as if her lips could make him float, finding himself levitating above their sheets.

"Make me yours, Ian, make me yours again," Daly said softly in his ear, as he completely lost every bit of control left in his being. Just then, several inches from the bed, floating above their reality as their bodies sweated and shuddered through that divine glory of sexual encounter, Ian poured himself into her. For several seconds, they both gasped and shivered until the throbbing slowly subsided and their bodies gently descended back to the bed. Completely tired and satisfied, the two remained together for a minute, as if they had been reviewing the fury of love and lust they had just experienced together again. It wasn't until Seba rang the cell phone for the fifth time that Ian decided to recover all his human sensations, which testified to the beating he had received less than thirty minutes before. Dalymar picked up her blouse, kissed him on the cheek and vanished.

∫∫Fifth

From the moment he entered Ian's apartment, the smell of blood mixed with Daly's scent was so strong and unique that Sebastián found it hard to concentrate on the story his brother was telling him. Just two minutes before he sat down, in order to medically attend Ian, he noticed the transient scars of a light drizzle that had just bathed the glass windows in front of the apartment, accentuated by the excess humidity and air conditioning. Inside, the temperature was much cooler than the infernal heat he felt when he walked out of his car. A little sweaty on his forehead and nose, he wiped the drops on his face with his hands and dried them, as well as he could, on his pants. Hanging over the walls of the main room were a pair of black and white cubist paintings. He glanced at them briefly, but his attention quickly turned to the center of the hall table, where there was a white vase of freshly cut red poppies. Those flowers were, without a doubt, Dalymar's favorite. As he sat down in front of them on a large leather chair, they made him smile with nostalgia. Once seated, and almost thirty-seven seconds before Ian walked over to greet him, he looked around and realized that everything else he hadn't yet carefully observed was in disarray. There were bloody footprints on the white tiles and pieces of toilet paper saturated with darker blood lying over the corner coffee table. The smell of blood was quite strong, not as potent as Daly's perfume, of course, but sharp enough to remind him of the thousands of procedures he had performed in the operating room, trying to stop some malignant gastrointestinal bleed. It smelled, in many ways, like when a perfumed woman had just ordered seven pounds of fresh beef in a butcher shop.

"Sebastián, are you there?" stammered Ian through sore teeth as he snapped his fingers, trying to wake him up.

Seba jumped a little and looked at his brother, nodding his head subtly in approval. In his trance, he was still thinking about the bad times in the operating room and the good memories he still had of his late sister-in-law.

With good reason, Ian did not want to confide the truth about his ridiculous battle in the shower that led to his current state. Instead he told his brother a story of how he had slipped awkwardly on his bathtub, but Seba didn't believe anything he said. To him, what made the most sense was that those bruises on his brother could only have been caused by a tremendous beating. "But who could have hit Ian so hard?" he wondered, "Could it be that that perfume that reminds me so much of Daly is from some other married woman? Could it be that her husband beat the crap out of Ian?" he thought.

As Ian continued to tell him how he crawled into his bedroom, Seba imagined every blow the jealous man had dealt him. Therefore, he decided to ignore his story and the "why" of the blows in order to pay more attention to the consequences. To him, if his suspicions were true and his brother had fallen for a woman, married or not, he deserved more than anyone else a fresh start. Ian was an adult; widowed and single. It had been more than four years since he lost Daly. It stood to reason that his older brother was ready to fall in love once again.

At that point, it had been almost twenty minutes since Sebastián had arrived at Ian's apartment to give him first aid. First, Seba disinfected his brother's wounds and put a simple butterfly stitch over his lower lip. He then examined him from head to toe and cautiously attended each of the lacerations, with an occasional one needing a few stitches, courtesy of the dissolvable sutures he had brought in his medical bag. After he was finished, he prescribed seven days of potent anti-inflammatories and muscle relaxants to lessen the pain. Once he finished acting as an emergency room physician, Seba got up and headed to the kitchen to make himself a cup of *café con leche*.

To his surprise, the kitchen was clean, with no trace of blood and was well painted in a grayish-white, almost like a surgical suite. Dr. Pérez-Fuertes meticulously poured sufficient coffee grounds into the grinding machine and pressed the red button to start it. Unintentionally, the smell of coffee reminded him of his beloved Doña Mama.

But who was Doña Mama? Well, in one sentence, she was a sixty-one-year-old Puerto Rican of Afro-Latin descend who had been baptized as Patria Jimenez. In more than one sentence, she had also taken on the task of raising the two children of a married couple who had enough money to pay for everything, including nurturing their kids. Patria came from a very poor family on the outskirts of the west coast of the island, near Aguadilla, and never got to finish high school, marry, or have children of her own. Despite her underprivileged upbringing, she was quite smart, she was loving and an excellent human being. She liked to pretend that Sebastián and Ian were partially hers and not, completely, her bosses'. Yes, they were her bosses', although anyone could argue that they treated her like masters treat a slave. Proof of this was that Doña Mama got up at exactly 6:00 a.m. every day she worked in the house to start brewing coffee, then collecting eggs from the chickens, washing the floors and scrubbing the bathtubs, dusting the furniture and beating the rugs. While breakfast was cooking, she normally sorted the laundry, picked up the dishes and threw away the leftovers, made the beds and fed the dog. Then, she cleaned the mirrors and contemplated the reflection of her misery, dressed the children and walked them to school, gave them a hug and two kisses on the head, used the bathroom and sighed deeply because of her sadness. Once she was again alone in the house, she would return to her chores and scrub the backyard, wash the clothes and hang them over the railing to dry, sweep the canopy and water the flowers, look up at the sky and smile in sorrow, thinking with much disappointment of the remote image of the happy girl she once was. Day by day, Doña Mama came to observe how, over forty years, those thick lines appeared under her eyes and became yellowish with time, along with the evolution of the 413,020 black and white curls that intertwined to create the gray hair that rested over her shoulders. Suddenly, the alarm would go off and she would look at the time, fetch the children and change their clothes, prepare the food and start dinner. At the same time, she would collect the clothes and fold them on the table, arrange the condiments and watch the dinner on the stove, answer the phone and listen to the complaints of Doña Mother, her boss. At night, she would visit the children in their room before bedtime and tell them a new fairy tale, in which she dreamed of being one of the fictitious characters and her real day to day life was a bit happier.

Unfortunately, neither Ian nor Seba ever knew how much Doña Mama suffered in the daily chores. They were also unaware of how much she sacrificed in order to stay with them, acting almost like a slave to their bosses, instead of a maid. Needless to say, the love she gave them had its effects, since both considered her more of a mother than anyone else, despite the fact that they bore Doña Mother's surname, "Fuertes".

A sharp noise made Sebastián jump and realize that the coffee was ready. He poured it, added milk and felt the steam as his lips approached the hot cup before letting the caffeine drip into his mouth. He was calmer now, but he still felt the screams of the insurer, while he sat in front of two of his lawyers, and listened to him in a thousand different ways say: "I hope this is the last of your stupid ideas or else I'll personally make sure they take away your medical license."

Seba ignored them. For his peace of mind, he preferred to repeat to himself a couple of times that it would not happen again. Although the truth was that the allegations against him were quite incriminating. For all intents and purposes, there were at least four precise reasons why he would probably be sued and this was without knowing whether the poor woman, for whom he had recently gotten into trouble, had survived. In monetary terms, his legal team had arranged to move all the properties in his name to a secondary corporation so that he would not be attacked, especially if anything like this were to happen again. In fact, if he were sued, the name of the corporation, "Los Doctores Fuertes," would most likely be the focus of attention. Still, the insurance company knew that no one else would give Sebastián medical malpractice insurance and, for that reason, their monthly payments were astronomical, which certainly benefited them. Incredibly, in many instances, doctors like Sebastián would either not go to court or simply settle under the table for minimal damages. So, almost hypocritically, the more mistakes and blunders he made, the higher his payments to his insurance company and the smaller his repercussions. At this stage of his career, well over half of his income went directly either to his malpractice insurance or to tax bills. For this reason, both parties knew that in the end everything between them would be forgiven, as long as Dr. Pérez-Fuertes continued to pay them.

The doorbell announced the arrival of a visitor and Seba, once again, couldn't help but jump in fright. This time, it was Doña

Mother's nose that was seven inches away from his own face. Sebastián looked at his brother and he seemed exhausted, tilting more towards the land of the dreams than the present. So, with no choice but to open the door, he breathed hard and grabbed the knob with a bad feeling. At that precise instant, he felt the nerve cells in his eyes adjust to maximize the amount of color that was about to escape through the entrance of the apartment. Once he opened the door, Sebastián found himself facing the image of the eighty-something-year-old woman who had brought him into the world.

Doña Mother was just under five foot and five inches tall. At her age, she still visited the "Country Club", or *Club de los Banqueros*, four times a week, not counting the activities and parties that were held sporadically. In addition to her social engagements, Doña Mother visited a beauty salon, called *El Popurrí*, on a bi-weekly basis. Today, Friday, she had just left the salon and decided to stop by Ian's house, which happened to be close by. Her hair had shown no signs of aging since her 35th birthday, when the world saw the simultaneous birth of her first child and her first gray hair. Since that ill-fated day, as she self-proclaimed the birth of her silvery hairs to be, she had accumulated such a concentration of dyes in her follicular strands that, every time she stepped out the door, she contributed a little to the global deterioration of the ozone layer.

Doña Mother dressed "fashionably", just as a movie star would in her golden years. Unfortunately for her, she had never set foot on the stage. Instead of singing opera or acting, she and her husband made their fortune by building one of the first pharmaceutical chains in the rural confines of central Puerto Rico. Once they achieved success by creating enough branches of that business network, they sold it, retired and traveled the world. For this reason, her clothing included designer clothes and glasses, Italian leather handbags, Swiss ceramic watches and luxury shoes.

Standing inside the apartment door, Sebastián had the opportunity to look at the image of his mother, with all the abdominal fat cushioning her and the 212 pounds of weight she carried on her feet. As she entered, Mother Pérez walked two steps and started speaking to him:

"Little Seba, my sweetheart, what a joy to see you here and not in that dump you call a bar. I mean, of course, that awful place you love, *El Bar del Murciégalo*. God is great and he knew I was coming here, that's why he got my two sons to be present, almost unconsciously, to see me..." Doña Mother continued, but Seba opted to shake his head and dust off that fake smile he used so much during his childhood years.

"Ian, guess who came to visit you," Seba shouted in a subtle, sarcastic tone as he interrupted his mother's muffled words.

Ian opened his right eye and looked at the elf's face. Ernie seemed to be staring at him, as if insinuating that he should feign sleep. Knowing that if he stayed in bed, he would still have to greet his mother the next day, Ian decided to get up and head for the bathroom to check on the ravages that *Hurricane Mr. Trickle* had left on his body. The reality was that he was battered and quite sore. Realizing that he was not going to make it out of his mother's interrogation alive, Ian decided to assume an attitude of complete alienation and answer all her questions abstractly. That is, when he came out of the bathroom, he would tell her, in detail, the harsh reality. Ten meters away, he felt his mother's words accelerating and drilling deeply into his ears. Ian trudged over to the sofa and sat down on his left side/buttock, which hurt less than the right.

"My Lord! But what happened to you, Ian, my darling? Who gave you such a beating? Don't tell me you and your brother went to *that bar* to have a few beers yesterday, because that would explain everything."

Ernie, standing on the bedside table, was part of the audience present at this melodrama played by Doña Mother. Several feet away from the conversation and through the half-open door to the living room, the more than two-foot-tall lamp-elf dropped his lower jaw as he witnessed the verbal battle that Ian and Sebastián had just started against Doña Mother. Ian began the onslaught by asking her how she dared to say such outrageous things. Seba then continued the attack by asking her if she was going senile or if she was just pretending to be. This caused his mother to regroup her troops and surprisingly launch back-to-back insults into both of their auditory systems, ranging from "not having given her grandchildren" to reproaching them that "she had paid for everything in their lives, including their first professional degrees and the roof over their heads." These repetitive phrases towards them were not one of those spur-of-the-moment sophisticated insults but more of a recurring theme which usually escalated the situation, as everyone knew they had a good degree of veracity and always left them both with a very sour taste. Thus, the two armies continued until the battle turned to gestures and not words. The anger of the trio reached such a degree that Ernie could only perceive the three of them moving their lips and emitting sounds far from any known language, as if they were surrounded by a deafening din that hid the real phrases they were shouting, performing an absurd pantomime which parodied something closer to a classic *Three Stooges* episode. After all the insults received from her children and after the counterattack she launched, Dolores Fuertes still did not understand why the world was so unfair to her, as she continued to pack every corner of Ian's apartment with insults.

Enraged, Sebastián got up from his chair and headed for the front door. That door was the chief escape from a building whose exterior was completely deteriorated by nostalgia. The structure, called *Les Pérez Apartments*, was originally designed by Engr. Ian Pérez-Fuertes and financed by his parents as a gift for passing his professional civil engineering license exam. However, he had never rented any of the other apartments to anyone. In fact, the building had never been inhabited by any human being other than Ian and Dalymar. Four years earlier, just before Daly's death, the structure had the rigidity and strength to withstand a category five tropical hurricane. Inside, the apartments were modern, quite comfortable to look at, though they had slowly filled with dust and whatever pest now called them home. On the outside, where they were once new they now looked somewhat shriveled. A closer look revealed only the vestiges of a lonely past. The exterior facade wore a green slime with blackish patches surrounding most of the eaves. The grass reached the knees of anyone who dared to explore it and it was inhabited by almost three battalions of insects trained to attack the intruders of that defeated castle. Outside it had a musty smell similar to that of earth in a container spread full of fungus. The walls looked rough, as if they were composed of a copper-edged papier-mâché that, at first glance, appeared to be randomly carved with water balloons. The apartment complex had three floors, each with three units for rent. Unfortunately, only the first floor, where Ian now lived, was ever inhabited. Water pressure was fairly steady in the building, but the walls had received more rain than a dam ready to collapse. The ivy, meanwhile, had already taken over the back of the structure and was flirting with the idea of climbing over to the roof to cover the entire *Les Pérez Apartments* complex. All this destruction lay around the second apartment of the first floor, #010b, encasing it like a weather-beaten walnut.

Keys in hand, Seba pressed the right button on his key fob, starting his car from a distance. An additional push of the left button released the front door locks. As he sat on his leather seat, he took just over sixty-seven seconds to calm down enough to start driving. The security cameras in Ian's building caught his red car as it faded into the distance.

This beautiful and sexy machine was equipped with all the unnecessary but luxurious details that would satisfy anyone rolling in money or, as the commercials called it, "anyone with exquisite taste." As he pressed his right foot on the accelerator, Sebastián could feel the 478 jolts of horsepower or the 356,588 volts rampaging inside the engine of his semi-automatic transmission car. First gear, no-clutch; second, accelerate; third, no-clutch; fourth, red light; stop, wait, no-clutch; first. Miraculously, while driving, he managed to forget that last encounter with Doña Mother. For a brief moment, he felt happy until, once again, he remembered the threatening letter:

You have one year to live

As he recreated that note in his mind, his skin became even paler than usual and the temperature between his ears rose to exactly 100.8° Fahrenheit. Progressively, he felt a thick sweat on his forehead, almost oily, which took over his whole body, turning into a rapid, substantial and progressive fever. Within seconds, he felt his chest trying to explode with every beat of his heart. "This must be a panic attack," he thought, "or maybe it's an arrhythmia, have I developed a bout of atrial fibrillation?" However, as he thought about his differential diagnosis, his lungs continued to try to evaporate every molecule of lactic acid that was piling up in his veins. Consequently, Sebastián felt nauseous, dizzy and immediately realized he was about to pass out, all while driving at approximately seventy miles per hour. Perhaps thirty seconds before losing his consciousness, Seba decided to pull over. As soon as he got off the main road, he felt everything around him spinning and his body floating frantically in the opposite direction to the earth's axis. In absolute synchronicity, his veins took on arterial functions, as if his blood was refusing the present and looking for a way to return to the past. His lungs stopped exchanging carbon dioxide for oxygen and lactic acid continued to accumulate exponentially. Consequently, he found himself surrounded by images of what could well be a movie based on the last days of his boring life, starting with a scene of Doña Mother screaming at him, leaking hurtful words through her false teeth; then he saw the coffee machine and Ian along with his bruises, smeared everywhere with fresh blood. Next, he caught the smell of the 15.75 beers he ingested with *Hiswife* and *Hislover* at *El Bar del Murciégalo*, while recalling the morning sun of Paris and his persistent mania for lurking around every corner of his apartment. Finally, his memory transported him to the side of his bed, after observing for the first time that clairvoyant note, authored by someone who claimed to augur *that* which there should be *no way* of anticipating. Floating in the memories of his bedroom, immersed more than a week away from the present, Sebastián looked around and watched the images of his life being projected on the walls of his room. They seemed like continuous, but fleeting, fractions of an untimely past. On the wall to his right, he relived his first birthday and the kiss of his first girlfriend. On the opposite wall, he traveled back to Aspen and the top of that towering, white mountain he once conquered while skiing. On the wall right before him, he could see his first medical school cadaver, whom they called *Veronica*, and whose lifeless ears had listened to him for long hours as he recited her anatomy, from head to toe. In a corner, somewhat disfigured, he caught a glimpse of Natalia and remembered how deeply he had loved her. Finally, behind his back, he saw himself once again graduating as a physician. In the distance, he could hear a male voice whispering a continuous message, providing the same dread he felt the first time he read the note and that would surely stay with him forever. The memory, in which that voice, so innocent yet so guilty, continued to read that message, sounded like a repetitive recording:

You have one year to live
You have one year to live
You have one year to live

When he opened his eyes, he found himself sitting behind the wheel in present time. He woke up sweaty and gasping for air even though his car had the air conditioning on full blast. He felt somewhat sick to his stomach, nauseous, but had enough strength to continue driving. Sebastián remained in his car for about nine minutes while he thought about everything he had just remembered. Subsequently, he scrubbed his face with both hands and began driving back to his clinic.

∫∫Sixth

"Hail Mary, full of grace...," said the young woman with her head bowed.

"... the Lord is with thee," replied the priest behind the screen in the confessional.

"Good morning, Father, I have come for I have sinned..."

Violeta Vanessa Contreau used to visit the confessional booth on a monthly basis to let Father Rodrigo know everything she had done in body and soul since her last visit. However, during that morning, Violeta was in the confessional for the fifth time that week. This was because since her mother's death she had not been able to erase a thorn of hatred she felt for the world and for being alive. Her wristwatch read 11:05 a.m. when she continued her confession.

"For having sinned yesterday. As soon as I got out of mass, I felt like eating a vanilla ice cream, so I went to Marta's ice cream parlor and bought the biggest one they sold."

"Tell me, dear, what's wrong with that?" asked the father in a reluctant tone.

"It's just that after I started eating it, I felt that rage that takes hold of me," Violeta paused and wiped her right cheek, on which a tear was rolling down.

"Go on, daughter," the Father murmured.

Miss Contreau was a good Catholic. Through the slits of the booth one could perceive a glimpse of her eyes, which were a mix of brown and green. Her dark black hair rested gently on her shoulders and on her face were freckles that spread like a faint drizzle of rain. At thirty years old, she was a fervent believer in the Roman Catholic Apostolic faith and that is why she was confessing, yet again, that morning. Overall, she was gentle, sincere, very genuine and intelligent. For some reason, at her age, she was still single, but it wasn't because she couldn't maintain a serious relationship, it was because she couldn't get away from being *everything* to her family, specifically to her late mother.

The Contreau family had arrived on the shores of Puerto Rico through the confabulations of fate. Their surname had a common ancestor from France/Spain, although this did not imply that its origin was extravagant. It was created by mere chance, similar to most existing last names. The history of this one began approximately 452 years ago in Paris, France, and has as its protagonist Violeta's great-great-great-great-great-grandfather, who was a man with a very short fuse. His lack of patience was seen in its maximum expression on the day when, in the middle of the village, armed with just his two fists, he beat up a farmer for laughing at his bad teeth. Such was the beating that it quickly became known in those parts as *Le Battement de Contró*, since "Contró" was the only thing that the badly wounded man could babble from his bed after such a pounding. Unfortunately, the blows received by that young man did not go unnoticed by his family. A few days after the event, all seventeen male members of the family armed themselves with nine picks, three axes, twelve sticks and each of the thirty-one sharp knives they possessed to try to disembowel the victimizer alive. For Violeta's great-great-great-great-great-grandfather, the exhaustive search by the poor farmer's family was an odyssey that prompted him to do what any human being would have done in the same situation: run away. And run he did. He did it with such speed that he left no trace behind him and, after almost seven months of flight, mounted on a very old but strong brown horse, he arrived in the north of Spain, very close to the area that today is the coast of San Sebastián. As the years went by, he managed to gallop further south, getting to know new towns and acclimatizing every day to the Catholic religion, which made him fall more in love with the area, until he finally settled in Madrid where he remained for many years. In the capital he learned the language to perfection and, in order to emphasize that he was not a coward, but a smart man who wanted to survive, he mixed his French descent with the reason why he left. As a result, he created his surname: Contreau Rios. He took it upon himself to forge with this name all his documents, especially those that authenticated him as a pure Catholic and native Spaniard. Thus, began the origin of his lineage and, many children later, almost 110 years before the current date, Violeta's great-great-grandfather decided to send his offspring to the Caribbean Sea in the hope of becoming rich in that new world called America. Now, four and a half centuries after *Le Battement de Contró*, Violeta was sitting down, about to continue with her confession that seemed insufferable to the priest.

"Well," continued Violeta with her story of sin, "I was so furious that I decided to experiment with the hardness of the glass that held my ice cream."

"Go on, daughter," the Father murmured again.

"So, I grabbed the ice cream cup and smashed it against the wall."

"But how on earth, knowing that Virgin Mary and Jesus Christ are always watching, were you capable of doing that?"

"I'm so sorry," said Violeta, her eyes close to overflowing with tears.

"Was anyone hurt?" asked Father Rodrigo in a more alert and less monotonous tone than at the beginning of the confession.

"No," she answered quietly, as another tear rolled down her left cheek.

"Violeta, let this be the last time you rebel and no more of these demonstrations of anger or aggression. You could have hurt someone and, if that had happened, you could have been arrested or God knows what else." The priest paused and inhaled an additional 650 milliliters of air, which was necessary to continue his reprimand to Violeta. "Now you will have to go to Marta's ice cream parlor, pay her for the damages, ask her many times for forgiveness and, as punishment, say a rosary to yourself."

Ms. Contreau did not hesitate. She apologized again to Fr. Rodrigo, promised never to do it again and left the church with a faint smile that only she could perceive. Instantaneously, she felt the guilt fade away as she walked out from paying Marta for the damages and asking her many times for forgiveness. The truth was that Violeta loved to pray and even more so when she had a good reason to do so. As a result, the additional recitation of an extra rosary seemed almost like a gift and not a punishment during that afternoon.

Since the death of her mother, Violeta did not feel like doing anything in her spare time, she felt sad, and incapable of feeling pleasure. At three o'clock in the afternoon, she would pick up her purse, her books and leave for home. Once there, she would look at the same portraits hanging on the walls, take a glimpse at one or two of the hundreds of books she had read a long time ago and sit in the living room watching the afternoon go by. Both she and her mother would leave the blinds closed, because they believed anyone, who wished them ill, could spy on them from the outside. For this reason, she was very cautious about where she went and to whom she talked. That day was the 0.01916th anniversary of her mother's death. Because of this, she had gone to the cemetery (accompanied by her rosary) to pray in honor of her memory.

Her mother's name was Rocío Costas and she was transported to the afterlife when she was almost seventy. Violeta still remembered her obituary, which her younger brother, Junior, wrote in her honor.

~~~~~~*~~~~~~

Rocío Costas de Contreau, mother, widow and friend. R.I.P.

Thank you for being the best thing in our lives. Your wise advice and words of faith will remain forever alive in our hearts. We are very grateful because, in you, God gave us a life full of love, dedication, commitment and, above all, humility. Mother, you have left your mark in every strand of our lives and fiber of our future. Today, through these lines, we want you to know that you can rest easy here in peace, on Puerto Rican soil. We will love you forever. See you soon.

~~~~~~*~~~~~~

Doña Rocío Costas de Contreau had five children: three girls and two boys. The boys were named Junior and Javier. The girls were Violeta Vanessa, Rocío Liz, and Alexandra. She was widowed at the age of fifty-five, when her husband died of pancreatic cancer less than two months after being diagnosed. As can be deduced from the death notice, she went out of her way to be an exemplary wife and mother to all.

Although they had all been close since they were little, as adults, things had changed. Nowadays, Violeta only talked occasionally to her brother Junior, since he was the only one living in San Juan. Her two sisters had married and moved to Florida, in the continental United States. Alexandra took care of her two children while her husband worked selling life insurance and Rocío Liz taught elementary school children, but never had kids of her own. Her other brother, Javier, had been involved in sports since he was a young boy, but ended up with a devastating injury to his right knee during high school that forced him to forget any dreams of making a living playing basketball professionally. As a result, he always felt unfulfilled in his life and never married. He worked unhappily as a loan officer at a bank and, for fun, wrote little poems and very short stories that he never published, leaving them frozen inside his computer for the rest of his life. Over the years, his depression over not becoming a professional athlete turned into bad habits and he slowly became addicted to food. By the time he was thirty-six, he weighed over 440 pounds and his sugars were so high that bees could feed on his sweat like a drizzle of pollen. Unbeknownst to him, he developed severe coronary artery disease and one bad day he went to sleep with abdominal pain, thinking it was indigestion, but never woke up, dying of a massive heart attack in his sleep. The family mourned him, Doña Rocío lived through the sorrow of burying both a husband and a son in her lifetime. Over time, her mother's memories of anguish were replaced by guilt. In essence, she felt forever responsible for never having helped him overcome his depression and food addiction, even though the fault was clearly not hers.

Her other brother, Junior, was a fiction writer by trade, although he also worked as a paralegal in a law firm to earn a living. As a not especially famous prose writer he had published some short stories in small magazines and a very good theatrical script that a company performed while he was still in college. He was married and had one small daughter, Camila, who was seven months old. He was of medium height, intelligent, quite kind and his hair was as white as his skin, despite not having many wrinkles on his face at forty years of age. Every year he dreamed of quitting work at the law firm and devoting himself completely to being a writer, imagining using the hundreds of ideas he had saved in a very old black notebook with the hopes of someday publishing his first novel. Unfortunately, the years continued to pass and expenses forced him to work harder as a paralegal to support his family.

Right after her mother's death, both Violeta and Junior had grown apart. In fact, they were so mad at each other that they preferred not to speak to one another. Predictably, her brother wanted to sell his mother's house to get the money from "his inheritance" so he could slow down at work and pursue his dreams of becoming a famous writer. But their mother had left their childhood home, in its entirety, to Violeta as a gift, since she had always cared for her and stayed by her side. After all the yelling and arguing, there was little Violeta wanted to know about Junior.

After becoming an orphan, she spent most of her nights longing for the simple life she had enjoyed while her parents were still alive; yearning those days where no one was sick and their obituaries hadn't been written. As a result, she felt utterly alone and saddened. She still missed her father, Mr. Martin Contreau, who was always very good to everyone. He worked as an accountant until his last days and provided as best he could for his family. One day, at the age of fifty-five, he woke up and, when he looked in the mirror, his skin was no longer pale but yellow. He felt no discomfort or abdominal pain, but his whole body, including his eyes, looked like the blondish mustard color of a moon when it is hanging very low over the horizon. The medical term he was missing to understand this bizarre new phenomenon was lacking in his vocabulary, but the textbooks use the word *jaundice* to describe it. That same week he went to the doctor and was immediately admitted to the hospital. Within a couple of days, he was diagnosed with pancreatic cancer. Unfortunately, by the time they caught it, the malignancy had already spread throughout his body; sadly, his liver, lungs and brain were compromised. The oncologists offered him several cocktails of palliative chemotherapy, but Martin declined, as they would at most give him a couple of extra months of life, framed by undesirable side effects. As a result, he decided not to treat it aggressively and to spend his remaining days at home with his family, in hospice. He died less than two months after the initial diagnosis, almost instantly and without much suffering, from a massive pulmonary embolism brought on by his cancer, while sleeping next to his wife, Rocío.

Despite feeling lonely and without much support from the little family she still had, Violeta did manage to entertain herself daily at her job. She was a full-time librarian, worked Mondays through Fridays, from 8:00 am to 3:00 pm. The pay was not much, but she was so fascinated by reading and the detailed organization of books that it was like paying her to enjoy her favorite hobby. Before her mother's death, Ms. Contreau used to arrive at the municipal library with a smile on her face and every day she left with a gratified expression.

She marveled at the secrets hidden behind each cover of the hundreds of thousands of books that surrounded her at work. Almost daily, she would close her eyes and remember the dream she'd had when she was only fourteen years old that had caused her to fall in love with literature for the rest of her life. In the dream, it was raining incessantly and drops kept falling on the metal frame of the window of her room. Consequently, Violeta woke up, put on her flip-flops and walk slowly to the window. Once she looked out and gazed into the distance, she was transfixed as she watched her house, along with the mango and avocado trees, the cars, bicycles and lamp posts floating above a thick sea of white letters that appeared to be forming words, verses and syllables. Softly, from the sky, twenty-six different symbols fell, capable of all kinds of permutations. The letters recombined, continuously, like sea snakes creating words and phrases that, for the most part, composed multiple sentences. She tried to read several of these lines, but as she read, the words disappeared from her sight. Ironically, in the distance, she could see millions of people trying to fish for those letters, attempting to catch a word that could be useful to express their feelings. In her dream, she could not recognize who the fishermen were, but she had the strange impression that they were writers, poets, or novelists, trying to rescue from that ocean of letters the perfect word or sentence that would complete their works. Violeta never forgot the images of their faces, full of joy.

After this prophetic vision, that much younger version of Violeta began visiting the library daily. She read Nasar's *Crónica Anunciada*, followed by Pirulo's *Víspera*, learned about the wit of *Babas de Satán* while devouring *La Ciudad de los Espejismos* and memorizing the great *Poema Número 19 + 1*. In short, as a teenager she enjoyed the delight of great Latin American geniuses, who carried with their writing the feelings of a continent. For this reason, she did not hesitate for a second when choosing as her profession the one that would give her the opportunity to spend her days in contact with the millions of fishermen who were still trying to catch the fruit and the essence of life in their writings, and who remained in her thoughts.

After leaving Marta's ice cream shop, where she went to ask for forgiveness, Ms. Contreau walked down the sidewalk, counting the 123... 124... 125... cracks that appeared every step of her way. Just as the count reached 142 cracks, she grew tired and began to think about what she would have for dinner. She watched three, four cars pass and, at the fifth car, she decided to venture across the avenue. Just before reaching the other sidewalk, she stopped, sensing a warning in her auditory system, which augured the desperate sound of a horn thirty...twelve...nine and then three feet away. Violeta turned 90 degrees to her right and, upon looking, found a red sports car just inches away from her black dress. Apparently, she had not really been paying close attention and had just attempted to cross the road without noticing the presence of a sixth car. Although she didn't suffer a scratch, she still received a huge shock. Her parasympathetic system began to act quickly and in a matter of seconds she was unable to control her symptoms. Violeta repeatedly tried to inhale that mixture of nitrogen, oxygen, water vapor and so on, but within fifteen seconds her lungs gave out, her heartbeat dropped to thirty-five beats per minute, her blood pressure collapsed below 70 mmHg (systolic) and her brain sent the obvious signal of partial fainting. At 11:35 a.m., the eldest daughter of Rocío Costas de Contreau collapsed onto the pavement. Unbeknownst to her, on that March morning, after having fainted, both Ms. Contreau and Sebastián would be reborn.

∫∫Seventh

It had been dormant for exactly twenty-one years. Since then, no one had wanted it to walk through their bodies, their lungs and even less through their immune systems. It was born, like everything else, from the DNA of some organism it usually inhabited. Although, to be born you have to live and certainly it had never been considered a living entity. The reason was obvious, it had very few characteristics that tied it to life. It had no metabolism, nor did it reproduce by itself and, even worse, there was no medicine to kill it, it could only eliminate itself and control its reproduction, since it did not live. In short, it needed a host to flirt with life. Its common name was Carlos, as it was so named by the Count of La Rioja in the year 1887. This aristocrat was very extravagant, so he christened at will all things, living or not, that roamed around his palace. This virus was no exception, as it had belonged to the richest and most powerful lungs in Europe. Its pedigree included the likes of Her Majesty Queen Victoria of England, Her Highness Queen Isabella II of Spain and even Napoleon Bonaparte, while he was emperor. In addition, during the late 19th century, its *curriculum vitae* was impressive enough to include the great family of the Count of La Rioja, which happened to be one of the most prominent Spanish lineages of the time.

While it "lived" in each of the thirteen members of the family, the viral cold Carlos was in charge of inducing a different symptom in each one of them. It was very important for it to contribute to the character of its host during its stay. It started with the little girl Sofía and, after wrestling with her defenses, Carlitos took hold of every fiber of her respiratory system. As a consequence, it caused fevers and muscle pain in the early days, but after that stage, it gave her the freedom to interact with the world. At that point, it would accompany her in the afternoons to the lake, while she played with her siblings and rode her bike around the big mansion. The most exciting part of the day, for the virus, was when it caused a state of apathy to most people. As the years went by this microscopic pest gradually grew tired of lurking in the bodies of every member of the family. Six years after starting *The Viral Marathon of La Rioja*, this uncommon cold crossed its finish line. Its last host, the Count of La Rioja, was the only one who noticed its long stay in the family and christened it *"Carlos"*. Once named, it decided to try its luck in other social strata and left as the guest of a cook who worked for the Count.

After several useless bodies and, after living with sinister people full of bad habits and manias, Carlitos arrived at Don Juan Contreau's grocery store through the Count's cook. It was the same Don Juan Contreau, Violeta's great-great-grandfather, who decided to embark for America. This is how the virus reached the new continent and, although no one knew it, it was the one that had the greatest influence on Don Juan's decision to leave Europe. Every night, the virus, which had taken hold of his left frontal lobe, made Mr. Contreau wake up in a cold sweat, telling him that if he did not sail away, he would die a poor man's death in his unknown grocery store in Madrid. These threats were more than enough to convince him. The years passed and the family grew until it entered the doors of Martin Contreau, along with his wife and five children. Incredibly, it went from handkerchief to useless surface, without invading any of its members, until it ended up hidden deep inside a small woman's coat that initially belonged to Rocío Costas de Contreau.

During the afternoon when Violeta was almost run over by a convertible, Carlos was in the right pocket of the coat Ms. Contreau had inherited from her mother. As hot as it was that afternoon, Violeta opted for the scent of her mother's memory regardless of the beads of sweat. At that point, that viral cold had been waiting for approximately 7,670.25 days for someone to dare to let it into their being. Violeta had been very close on several occasions, but something always happened that prevented the disease from taking over her thoughts, her body and her feelings.

When she opened her eyes, Violeta found herself breathing in thick, ash-flavored air. The sky was dark, cloudier than it had been just thirty seconds before, when suddenly she heard, "Are you okay? I'm a doctor, I can help you." Although it was in perfect Spanish, her native language, the only thing Violeta could decipher from those two sentences was the word doctor. It took the lady a couple of seconds to focus on the blurry figure who was talking to her. But, once she managed to sharpen her vision, Violeta perceived a slight flow of current over her body, which marked the genesis of a metabolic pathway within her cells. Lying on the pavement, she felt the invasion of those brown eyes that studied her closely. The woman blinked repeatedly in the hope of seeing him disappear, but nothing happened. Sebastián's gaze was exposing Ms. Contreau to an invisible radiation, which penetrated deep into her skin. As a consequence, her epidermis began to change color, almost acquiring the tone that warm milk gifts to brewed coffee. Violeta felt a deep burning and, looking at herself, noticed the warmth of her new complexion. In unison, her body began a homeostatic process aimed at trying to counteract that change and, thus, forever remain identical. The reality was that none of this mattered. Regardless of how hard her veins tried to avoid that conquest, the damage had already been done: the excessive melanin had taken control over her skin. From that minute on, Violeta became someone else. Not only physically, but also sentimentally. Despite her subclinical depression, Ms. Contreau had just been transformed into someone more human, a person who could be loved and expected to give love in return. The only detail was that the change could not be fully perceived by the masses, as her skin color remained identical, very pale, in the eyes of the world.

"Doctor?" asked Violeta, but she realized that the question was really unnecessary. She didn't care whether she knew the answer or not.

Gingerly, Sebastián reached over and touched her cheek. As he did so, he noticed that it was cold.

"Yes, and I could take you to my office for observation or take you to the ER for urgent medical care," said Seba.

Violeta said yes with her head, but, in a matter of several seconds, closed her eyes again. Sebastián took her pulse and counted her breathing. Physically she showed only a superficial wound on her right ankle as a result of the fall. He was sure he hadn't hit her, but he was still extremely worried about what might happen to her if he left her in the middle of the road. The street was completely deserted, even though it was almost noon. Deep down, Seba knew that the answer to his question of "whether or not I should bring her in and observe her in my Gastroenterology office?" was obvious: "No, of course not, call an ambulance, let them take her to the hospital, don't drive her to your office." Still, almost by instinct, he decided to ignore his impulses and do the exact opposite. Next, he picked up her purse and, lifting her gently, managed to place Violeta inside his vehicle, on the passenger seat.

On the way to his office, Sebastián took care, using his best techniques, not to hit any of the craters that were surrendering to his tires. Arriving at his office, he parked and stopped to listen to the deafening silence of that high-pitched *tinnitus.* Sitting behind the wheel, he felt an unavoidable urge to stare at Violeta. In order to satisfy his desire, Sebastián rotated his head on the vertical axis of his neck, at eighty-seven degrees counterclockwise, and carefully observed this stranger passenger of his strolling through the world of dreams. His doctor's instincts knew that he had not caused her any serious physical harm, but he preferred to avoid an unnecessary lawsuit or, worse, going to jail for not providing his services. Besides, there was something about her that had caught his attention from the moment he observed her laying on the ground, something tender and warming that gave him a desire to help her.

Inside of his office, everything smelled new, especially since they had just moved in a few days ago. This was the first week they had been there. The interior looked like something out of an Italian boutique. The ceiling and walls were white and the floor was constructed of crystalline looking grayish tile. On the back wall, it had three gigantic paintings positioned in such a way that they gently set the mood in the waiting room. Upon arrival, Seba opened the door and entered without looking at Natalia, Don Juan, María, Mrs. Gutiérrez, Gabriel, Facundo, Miguel, Agapita Fernández, Dr. Avilés, Lola López, Engineer Valdés, Tomás, José, Arcadia Díaz, José, Elaine, Yary, Javier, Omar, Daniel and Inés. He passed one, two, three and, at the fourth door, he decided to turn, extend his right hand and open it. The fourth door belonged to the observation room where, in addition, they had several wheelchairs in case of emergencies. Once he grabbed a chair, he went out and rewound the entrance scene, as he ignored Inés, Daniel, Omar, Javier, Yary, Elaine, José, Arcadia Díaz,

José, Tomás, Engineer Valdés, Lola López, Dr. Avilés, Agapita Fernández, Miguel, Facundo, Gabriel, Mrs. Gutiérrez, María, Don Juan and Natalia... again.

Judging by her inability to open her eyes, Violeta appeared to be completely exhausted. In fact, it was somewhat worrisome that she could not stay awake after passing out. Especially since she was not faking her state of consciousness, her body was really unresponsive. Sebastián placed her in the wheelchair with the gentleness with which a butterfly is placed on a child's fingers. He calmly pushed her into the observation room and placed her on a reclining bed in the corner of the room.

Nata didn't take long to arrive. As soon as she saw Violeta, she pulled Seba by the arm and asked him: "Who the hell is that?"

Sebastián already knew beforehand that Natalia was not going to like the story in which he almost ran over an unknown woman and that, because of this, he had to make sure that nothing would happen to her, even more so when, to achieve this, he took the almost unconscious lady to his clinic, instead of calling an ambulance. Even before he began to tell her, during the four seconds of silence between Natalia's "... the hell is that?" and Sebastián's future "Calm down, Natalia, what happened was...", Dr. Pérez-Fuertes knew that he was going to get reprehended for: having arrived late to the clinic, not saying hello when entering, not to mention having brought a stranger that he had almost run over. However, "what's done is done", thought Seba, and began his manipulated story of the truth.

"Calm down, Natalia, what happened was that Ian called me early this morning, while I was on my way here from the insurance company's office because, supposedly, he had fallen in the bathtub. Well, you know family comes first, as you always say, so I went and fixed him up, but, on the way back, to my blessed luck, Doña Mother arrived and gave us both a hard time, so I stormed out of Ian's apartment like a fury. On the way back here, a lady, *that one*" as Sebastián pointed to Violeta "jumped in front of my car and I almost ran her over. Fortunately, I was able to stop in time and didn't hit her, but I brought her along anyway, just after asking her permission, to observe her for several hours and thus avoid more problems with the insurers."

"And how is everyone?" asked Natalia.

"I don't know," said Seba, "I'm almost certain she has no physical injury, except for the laceration on his ankle, but apparently her nervous system has not overcome the shock and *vasovagal syncope* that caused the fainting."

"I don't care how *she* is, but rather how are Ian and your mother doing?" Natalia answered loud and fast, with hints of anger in her voice.

"Ohhhh! Doña Mother is as ridiculous and obnoxious as always. On the other hand, Ian is doing better. I patched up a few superficial wounds, put butterfly stitches in his right lower lip and a few silk dissolvable sutures in several additional places. I also gave him some oral anti-inflammatories and muscle relaxants to bring down the swelling from the bumps. Personally, it looked to me like he was beaten up because of some romantic triangle, because there was an unbearable, very strong, womanly smell mixed with blood in that apartment."

Natalia smiled as she remembered the scent of Daly from Ian's apartment, although this moment of peace did not last long as, as she turned around, she remembered that there was a rather attractive woman lying on the bed in the observation room.

"I'm not even going to tell you what to do. What's more, in case your brain has gone on vacation, that woman you brought in has not signed any kind of consent for you to bring her here or for you to take care of her medically; so, by all means, she could easily sue you or even accuse you of kidnapping. But what am I saying? You already know that; you're an expert on lawsuits. You better put on your white coat and start seeing patients, there is a waiting list of seventeen people. I'll get the nurses to open a medical record, take her vitals, put her on a monitor and at least make sure you are covered in case something is wrong with this unknown woman." Natalia turned around and left the room after closing the door as quietly and forcefully as she could.

Sebastián complied with her order and put on his medical gown. Even though he knew his nurses could collect her vitals, he decided to examine her and do it himself before he started seeing patients. Stethoscope in hand, he walked to the examination bed where Ms. Contreau-Costas was lying. Upon arrival, he found his nurse, Tatiana, standing by the vital signs machine. "Thank you, Tatiana, I'll take care of this patient, could you put the next person in an exam room," Sebastián said.

Once alone, he reached out his hand with the goal of palpating her pulse and noticed that it was consistently clocking in at sixty beats per minute. Subsequently, he extended his stethoscope and placed it on his patient's chest; breathing sounded normal, the heart sounded strong and without any apparent murmur. He examined her head and saw no bruising or bleeding that needed tomographic imaging. He touched her cheek and felt reassurance with the warmth of her skin. He then took her blood pressure: 110/70 mmHg and her respirations, sixteen per minute, were coming in at ninety-nine percent oxygen saturation (without any supplementation). Everything about her vital signs was quite comforting. Sebastián then picked up the phone in the observation office and called Tatiana again so that she could write the vitals in her medical record (as Nata had suggested), place a cardiac monitor and document the visit.

"What is her name and what is her date of birth?" asked Tatiana.

"Great questions, well, I don't know yet, call her Jane Doe, date of birth 1/1/1991," answered Dr. Pérez-Fuertes, recognizing that it was somewhat absurd that he still had no idea who she was.

As soon as he hung up the phone, Violeta opened her eyes, causing an atypical reaction in Sebastián's skin. Automatically, he sensed her heat as it traveled over his being, spreading through his right hand, past his elbow until it reached his neck, where it split into two hemispheres. The burst of heat that subdivided towards the cranial part of his torso took care of spreading through every space within Sebastián's consciousness and subconsciousness. On the other hand, the blast that spread through the caudal hemisphere, towards his chest, went down his internal jugular vein and found its way into his heart, where it spread through his right ventricle and lungs, mixing vigorously with oxygen, until it reached his left ventricle and exited through his aorta to the rest of his body. Once that heat took control of his being, Violeta closed her eyes again and fell, once more, into a deep blissful sleep.

Sebastián was speechless, but equally intrigued by that handful of sensations. Several seconds later, he reached for his first aid kit and dressed the ankle wound of Ms. Contreau, who still remained a stranger to him. He then tucked her in with two blankets and headed to his office. Using a small monitor and a camera, his nurses continued to watch over her for the rest of the afternoon.

"Next." Was heard at the front desk. Patient coming, patient going. "Next." Constipation. "Up the dosage of that ineffective medicine." "Next." Hemorrhoidal bleeding. "Nothing serious to worry about, increase the fiber and put this steroid ointment around where it hurts the most." At a rapid pace, the afternoon continued, as he watched one patient after another coming in, telling him their immediate gastrointestinal sorrows, and passing through with the hopes of living a less painful life. During that afternoon, only one of the patients caught his attention, a young woman who always did at each previous visit. Her name was María and she was twenty years old. She was diagnosed at birth as congenitally deaf, but her audible speech status was fascinating; especially if she chose to pick you.

"Good afternoon, doctor," María said to Dr. Pérez-Fuertes without moving a single segment of her lips or her hands. The situation was so atypical and odd that even the mother, Mrs. Gutiérrez, who was sitting next to her, could not hear a syllable of the conversation. Because of this, Seba was not surprised when her mom began to tell him how María had been feeling during these last few days, without any kind of exaltation for having heard her deaf daughter speaking loudly. As part of the scene, the young woman was seen signing to her mother and, later, the mother was observed translating for her. Sebastián was not totally shocked by the situation, mainly because he had cared for her before. She suffered from *Crohn's disease*, which is a chronic gastrointestinal inflammatory problem.

"How are you, María? I imagine you must be tired of waiting for me," said Sebastián kindly.

The mother began to speak, but, at the same time, Sebastián heard the young woman reply:

"I waited a long time, but don't worry, picking up Violeta was a good deed and you will soon see that it was worth it."

"Violeta?" thought Sebastián, "could that be her name? And how does she know? Is it possible that she knows her?" The doctor chose not to ask, he knew that she would not answer him by voice and, worse, he would pass for insolent in front of Mrs. Gutiérrez. For that reason, he reviewed her recent labs with inflammatory markers, made notes of the symptoms described by her mom/interpreter and finally prescribed a newer immunological agent that the nurse would give her before she left, with the hopes to try to bring down the inflammation in her intestines. Although she didn't converse with many people, when María spoke (as if she was using her larynx), her words infused an odd air in her receiver. It was actually kind of creepy, since the people she communicated with didn't see her moving her lips or signing, they simply heard her in their minds. As a result, no one ever talked about this phenomenon, it was an open secret that everyone preferred to omit; especially because no one liked to feel like a madman who heard voices where it was scientifically impossible for them to come from.

Dr. Pérez-Fuertes finished seeing all of his seventeen patients at 4:55 p.m. Right after, he thanked Natalia and the team for the day's work. Next, he took off his gown, his stethoscope and passed by the room where Violeta was. As he entered, he felt very cold, so he put his hands inside his pockets, took a deep breath and approached her.

"Violeta," said the doctor, as he looked at her right hand, which was wearing a bracelet with her name on it, confirming what María had told him.

She woke up and for the first time said more than one word.

"Where am I?" she asked, half frightened and in a sleepy voice.

"I'm the doctor who picked you up off the street after you passed out. You're now in my office. Do you remember anything about what happened?"

Violeta moved her head, very slightly, diagonally, letting Seba know that she wasn't sure if she remembered his face or if her memory was narrating a dream.

"Who are you again?"

"My name is Sebastián, I'm the doctor you almost accidentally caused to run you over," he replied as he smiled.

Ms. Contreau remained silent as she tried to register the last sentence Sebastián had just uttered.

"I am so sorry, but my memories seem so fragmented. Probably because I hit my head," Violeta paused again, moistened her lips and continued, "Do I know you? How do you know my name? I apologize a thousand times and may the Lord repay you for all you have done for me. Really, I didn't realize that I crossed the street without looking, only Virgin Mary and all the Saints know what could have happened if it hadn't been for you."

"Well, we were very lucky that nothing happened. You only had a laceration on your ankle and I took care of that for you. As for the fainting, it was probably the result of poor ventilation from the scare and shock, followed by a *vasovagal* fainting episode, but you don't have any lumps or signs of head trauma, so we can rule out any additional damage. For the time being, be sure to rest and take the sedatives I will give you. The consultation and medical care are, of course, both free. And, with respect to your name, well you just got your bracelet to thank for giving your identity away, with a very nice, *Violeta*, written in cursive script."

She smiled, grabbed his hand and kissed it as if he were Pope John XXIII. Sebastián liked the gesture, smiled back and stroked her head as if she were a child. Apparently, she somewhat remembered almost everything, was essentially unharmed, and thus Seba had just saved himself any legal and ethical repercussions against him. Interestingly, he didn't think he had seen her bracelet until a couple of minutes before waking her up. Logically, the only thing that made sense to him was that perhaps he had imagined his conversation with María and, subconsciously, had seen and then forgotten his companion's bracelet, which definitely gave away her first name.

Although she tried to insist on calling a cab to pick her up, Sebastián convinced her to let him take her home. As they got into the car, they both felt a bond that was hard to explain. He chatted at the beginning of the ride and Violeta continued, for her part, from the middle of the ride to her house. They talked about everything except their past. It was as if they had started a conversation of two individuals who have no sad memories, but a joyful present to carry on. When they arrived in front of her house, neither of them dared to end the conversation. Sitting in the car, they talked about books and interesting facts, chatted about myths and casual stories. They told each other their hobbies along with an occasional happy memory, until the clock struck 9:51 pm. At that moment, Ms. Contreau realized that she had to go in, as she was never used to being out so late. Violeta looked at Seba and said:

"Well, thank you for sparing my life this afternoon." She paused, and they both smiled, "But thank you, above all, for caring about me, even though you didn't know me. May God always bless you!"

"Don't worry, it was my pleasure," said Seba from the driver's seat. "Actually, I couldn't be happier to accidentally meet you and I'm so glad you're okay."

As she opened the door, right before she stepped out of the car, Sebastián looked down and blurted out the obvious question that had been plaguing him since the halfway point of the ride.

"Would it be possible to see you again, not in a chaotic and unexpectedly medical way?" asked Seba, while his face reflected a glow of nervousness and accentuated his frightened voice.

Violeta paused, fell silent and Sebastián began to feel the terrifying urge of wanting to become invisible so he could escape from that awkward moment. Then he spoke again and said:

"I mean, if it's no problem. Tomorrow is Saturday, so I thought it would be a good day to go for a walk along the *Paseo de la Princesa*, if you're feeling better. I promise not to run you over."

Dr. Pérez-Fuertes knew very well that the best thing for Violeta was to rest. In fact, he himself had recommended that in his office. Ms. Contreau, for her part, remained mute and reflective. As soon as he made the recent invitation to go for a walk the next day, Seba felt that previous urge to disappear grow faster, almost exponentially. Of course, all these feelings vanished when he heard that sweet voice, which would remain in his ears for the rest of the night.

"I don't know, maybe it would be nice if I went for a walk tomorrow, Saturday, around 11:00 a.m., and, by surprise, I met someone like you. That way I could breathe some fresh air and leave something for fate to embellish my afternoon," Violeta answered with good humor.

"Understood. Maybe I'll do the same tomorrow at the same time then," Sebastián replied.

Afterwards, they both smiled and said goodbye. Although neither had bothered to ask each other's last name, the two left happily, as this gave them something to talk about on their first official date.

♪♪Eighth

It was during the winter of the dark years when Samuel Luis Pérez met Dolores Fuertes. At that time Samuel was a young soldier who had enlisted at the age of eighteen for military service. He never received any formal education. In fact, he did not even finish high school before signing up for the U.S. Army. At fifteen years old, he went to work on the San Juan docks to support his family until he was old enough to wear his fatigues and a pair of boots. Fortunately for him, his tactical education was good and adequate, even though he had to work like a mule to become "somebody" in the military. He started out as plankton, essentially polishing floors with his toothbrush, serving as the lowest food link in the evolutionary ladder. Then he used his toothbrush to clean toilets and later did the same with the company's millions of pieces of junk. He cleaned so many useless surfaces with his toothbrush that, in time, Samuel became so proficient with it that he became the only person, living or dead, able to use it for eating, cooking, bathing, floating, writing, threading, sitting, thinking, combing his hair and, when he had time, even brushing his teeth. Despite his many extravagant polishing skills, it wasn't until Private Pérez began performing tasks without using his toothbrush that he began to gain respect within his military company.

During his first year as a soldier, Samuel managed to remain under battalion guard for seventy-two hours without sleep or a bite to eat, surviving only on water. A month later he earned a medal for rifle shooting by recording the best marks in the entire company. This, together with the fact that he was submissive, obedient and efficient in his duties, greatly pleased Colonel Morales-Borrero, Samuel's troop leader. So, when his squad had to go out on their first secret mission in Central America, his colonel chose him as one of his key soldiers to complete the military attack and promoted him from Private First Class to Corporal ranks.

In Central America, his platoon did everything it was willing to do without asking many questions. At that time, the world of warfare was lived without many repercussions or consequences. This was true for the U.S. military as well as for all countries with good military intelligence and technical capabilities. Thus, it was not widely known that they detonated bombs in spy installations, which in reality ended up being schools or some other house that sheltered innocent children. Snipers took out important targets and killed dozens of people in order to continue to dominate those "underdeveloped" countries. As I said, it was a different time of war. There were no global online news outlets or "live feeds" on social media. At the end of the mission, Corporal Pérez was promoted all the way to sergeant ranks and then given a medal for valor for having saved three soldiers who were attacked by the anti-American enemy with the help of his fine sharpshooting skills. In an accelerated way, this young military man was having a brilliant career in the U.S. Army and it was precisely around that time that the future mother of Sebastián Luis and Ian Samuel met him.

Cecilia Beltrán, Ceci, was Dolores Fuertes' best friend. The two grew up together and studied in the same classroom until they graduated from high school. They were like sand and sea. There was no social event they did not attend together. Two months after graduating from high school, Ms. Fuertes received a visit from Ms. Beltrán.

"Hello, pretty girl, how are you?" Ceci asked.

"I'm fine, but just really, really bored."

"Well, Dolores, I have the solution to take your mind off that boredom and believe me when I say you will love it."

After hearing this, Dolores became excited. The last time she had gone out with Ceci she had met Marcos, a vibrant young man who had almost kissed her, although she had not seen him again after that night. So, without even asking where they were going, she accepted the invitation. The last thing she heard from Cecilia before she closed the door of her house was: "Dress like we are going to the prom again."

Dolores took this suggestion seriously and applied her make-up meticulously. With each brush stroke on her face, she was careful not to leave a single wrinkle. The iron did the same on her long, black dress and she combed her hair in a simple but elegant knot. Her dress had a slight neckline and her back was exposed to the waist. The rest of that black silky outfit ran closely around her form until it reached her thighs, separating her petite figure from her calves to her feet.

After applying her makeup and getting dressed, Dolores put 0.15 fluid ounces of her favorite perfume on her skin, while making every effort not to wake anyone so they wouldn't find out she was going out without permission. At 8:02 p.m. Dolores was already out of her house. She used the back door when she left, which as a matter of good neighborly custom, no one ever locked. She knew exactly where to go to meet Cecilia since they both had a common meeting point for these escapades. Once she reached the fifth mango tree by the corner park, she whispered "Ceci" and waited until she heard her.

"I'm here," answered Cecilia, who was dressed in blue.

"Hey, I thought you hadn't arrived yet," said Dolores a little excited. "Where are we going?"

"No need to know too many details, silly girl, just follow me," she said.

Subsequently, the two young women walked alone along that deserted road. As they strolled, they were watched by the stars, three beetles and a few hundred little coquí frogs that shouted with joy "how much they loved their island." At half a mile from their final destination they began to hear the joyful roaring of a party.

From the street, the house they were heading to looked like something out of a Puerto Rican version of *The Great Gatsby*. It had two stories and its architecture resembled that of a piano built of lime, stone, sand and Ponce cement, like most of the structures built in Puerto Rico at that time. The imposing structure was painted in a light cream color. From its outskirts one could see its magnificent state of care. Its garden was meticulously landscaped and adorned the house's roundel with huge stones and a large fountain at the foot of the entrance which connected with an outside pool. In the distance, music could be heard coming from inside the house, it was soft, but suitable for dancing. The mansion had at least twenty-five windows from the angle at which Cecilia and Dolores were standing. Each one of the blinds dripped a white light that, along with several sighs and casual smiles, made for a good prelude to the party.

After arriving at the front of the house, the question was not whether they should enter or not. Actually, the question was how to avoid being sucked in by its charm, once they crossed through that half-open door. The girls initially hesitated to enter, until Cecilia grabbed Dolores by the hand and started the journey towards the entrance of that huge party. Inside it was all *BBB* (*Baile, Botella y Baraja:* Dance, Drink and Gamble), which was an old colonization idea, based on the fact that an entertained cultural collection of people, such as the ones that lived in our island, do not usually rebel against their master. Of course, all the Puerto Ricans inside that party were loyally mesmerized by the *BBB.*

Upon entering, no one, not even a waiter, demanded credentials or an invitation. There were thirty-four round tables with white tablecloths with six chairs each. In addition, twelve couples were dancing on the central dance floor and another two right next to their tables. Most people did not even notice the two girls' discreet entrance. Even though they knew no one, they were not intimidated. With a lot of effort but very little embarrassment, Cecilia and Dolores acted as if they had been invited to the party and settled at one of the two completely empty tables.

Once seated, the reason for the celebration became evident. They had joined a party for U.S. Army soldiers who had just arrived back from battle. Among so many soldiers with medals on their chests, there was every flavor of rank, from sergeants and privates, to colonels, nurses and generals. Amidst that tide of strangers, the lonely ladies remained motionless in their seats for a long time, until twenty minutes turned into a long, thick wait. Without realizing it, the more bored they became, the more they began to converse in very low voices.

"Cecilia, I'm getting bored," Dolores whispered while feigning a ventriloquist smile.

"I know, me too. Let's see if one of these hicks dares to ask us to dance, if not, we'll see if we can have a few drinks, even if it's only water."

A quarter of an hour later, the plan was not going smoothly. Not only were they still not being asked to dance, but they didn't even dare to stop for drinks. Slowly, they felt imprisoned in their own ball gowns, with no hope of enjoying the huge party their eyes were witnessing.

"Good evening," said a man from over their shoulder.

As they turned around, they found the voice belonged to a dark-haired soldier, dressed as an officer, who was about six foot six inches tall, well-built, with a pronounced chin and a face so wide that he looked more like a trained bulldog than a soldier. He had brown eyes and a very short black hair that was barely noticeable above his tight forehead. Just between his eyebrows were the hints of a flattened nose, which hung over his face as if it had been misplaced. The girls were thrilled, not because of the beauty of that *doggy* hunk of manhood, but because such an action showed that they were not transparent to the human eye. Fortunately, that corpulent man was not alone. Standing just behind him was a not so tall soldier, his face showing total intimidation in the presence of the ladies.

"My friend and I are both soldiers. We are celebrating the arrival of our combat squad," said the man with the broad nose and thick fists. "We were sitting in the left corner of the room and wondered how two girls as beautiful as you could be alone." The girls smiled, thoroughly enjoying his attention.

"Well, actually, we were waiting for two gentlemen to approach us and ask us to dance," said Cecilia with a seductive tone, fluttering her eyelashes.

These words triggered a great emotion within the chests of the soldiers. In fact, so great was it that, without even thinking about it, the broad-fronted officer extended his hand, saying, "Well, here are two gentlemen willing to treat you like princesses tonight."

Ceci then left for the dance floor with the larger of the soldiers and Dolores remained seated next to that other man who, at first glance, seemed mute. He had cinnamon-colored skin and small cheeks, which were very skinny and bony. That poor soldier could not have looked more like a sad, poor wrung-out lizard. Both his arms and chest were small, very different from Cecilia's "bulldog" dance partner. The man sitting next to Dolores had straight, neat teeth, with a very soft gleam just behind his lips. Below his nose was a fringe that seemed to hint at the incipient stages of a frustrated mustache. His hair was brown and retained some golden curls, brought on by the sun. In short, both his appearance and his gestures reflected that he was too nervous to start a conversation.

"Heh, hum, Hel-lo, I'm Samuel," stammered the scurrying lizard to the surprise of everyone, including this narrator.

"Hello," replied Dolores, equally surprised.

"Just for the records, I'm not very good at these things, but I'm a real gentleman and I, I, I'd like to ask you to dance. As I told you, my name is Samuel, it's nice to meet you," he said with a sincere tone.

Even though he said this, the man made no move to get her out on the dance floor, which is why Dolores had to take the initiative, otherwise she was going to remain seated and without a dance partner for the rest of the evening, as the presence of this Samuel was sure to scare off any other suitors.

"Well, let's go and dance." Dolores Fuertes extended her hand and felt for the first time, in her eighteen years, the warmth of a man who was really worth it.

"Sure," Samuel replied and led her to the dance floor.

Sgt. Samuel L. Pérez was dressed as an officer and wearing the annoying medals that his future son, Sebastián, would feel in the somniferous reproduction of this moment. As they danced, he breathed in her perfume while holding her in his arms. He contemplated her gaze and tender smile, perceived the touch of her fingers and soft caresses. The night was magical, so much that he could swear he was floating, with no idea of how many inches away he was above the ground. "She is stunning," Samuel thought, "she's quite a princess." Yes, she had a very delicate figure; her complexion was somewhat tanned and her eyes were framed by voluminous lashes. The lady wore an exquisite perfume, she smelled of orchids assorted with the fragrance of a woman's pleasure. Her neck was unique and adorned by a faint mole that served as a preamble to the delicate purple necklace, with silver accents, that hung tenderly over her shoulders. The dance floor was drenched in glitter and the night showed no signs of ending. The music kept playing, the room continued to spin in unison, while Samuel's body experienced the pressing symptoms of love as it flooded the heart of a lonely man. And so, it went on, until the clock struck 11:51 p.m. At that precise moment, Dolores leaned close to his ear and whispered:

"I have to go. Will you walk me home?"

"Sure, no problem," Samuel replied, "it will be my pleasure."

Then, little by little, everything began to stop. The ground did the same by no longer rotating and becoming opaque, while the music became disfigured until only the sound of a bomb blasting over a children's school, located in Samuel's memory, could be heard.

"Are you alright?" asked Dolores and Samuel nodded his head as he recovered from his depressive trance.

As soon as they were out the door Dolores grabbed his hand to feel safer as he escorted her. Together they walked silently down that dirt, unlit walkway that led to Dolores' house. Like her and Cecilia on their way to the party, Samuel and Dolores also had chaperones as they walked back. They were still watched by the silent stars on their belt of Orion, they listened again to the singing of the coquís as they were illuminated by that trio of beetles that still watched them. A sixth of a mile from Ms. Fuertes' house, Samuel began to talk for the first time since they stopped dancing.

"My full name is Samuel Luis Pérez and I am a sergeant in the United States Army," he said, his voice a little shaky. "What's yours?"

"Dolores Fuertes, that's my name," she answered, realizing that she had not even told him her name despite having danced with him for several hours that night.

Although Samuel had told her his military rank, Dolores was not at all impressed with his uniform or his title of sergeant. In fact, Dolores didn't know the difference between sergeant, colonel or private.

"Dolores..., a beautiful name, worthy of a delicate lady," replied Samuel, a little surer of his words. However, he knew deep inside the direct English translation of her name was almost exactly "*Dolores*: Pains" and "*Fuertes*: Strong", "Strong Pains or Painfully Strong?", he thought to himself, with the infinite certainty of never, ever reproducing that train of thought.

"Thank you, but I prefer to be called Doly."

"No problem, Doly, that's what I'll call you."

After these words they continued talking until they reached the back of Doly's house. There they each sat on the two swings which hung from a gigantic, flamboyant orange tree. Under the darkness of night, they talked for long hours, until after three o'clock in the morning. Two minutes after that time they said goodbye and promised to see each other at dawn the next day.

The next day they saw each other again. The same thing happened every night until, after a couple of weeks, they increased the dosage of their companionship. By then they saw each other every night at the same times, between 12:00 and 3:00 am. After several months of seeing each other almost in secret, they decided to change the visiting hours to dusk, so that their relationship could be more "legitimate" and less conducive to sleepy mornings.

During some of these late afternoons they used to walk around town with Doly's younger sister, serving as a disguised chaperone, so as not to cause any kind of scandal about their unannounced courtship. However, in the late weekend evenings they would meet, once again, in the Fuertes family's shadowy backyard, where they would sit on the two swings hanging from that flamboyant orange tree to talk and kiss until exhaustion overcame them. One of those nights, six and a half months after they met, they found themselves alone, giving each other a little more than they had ever given each other. In the dark, they started kissing until, rhythmically, their lips became wetter and more passionate. Even though both swings were less than eighteen inches apart from each other, that small separation became too distant. Slowly, but progressively, they felt an immense march of heat and desire. Without realizing who started what, Samuel and Dolores found themselves standing still, kissing in a continuous, breathless and rapid fashion, feeling a thick sweat rising from the tops of their legs, passing through every corner of their breasts and stopping at their lips. Samuel had his hands around Dolores' lower back and Miss Fuertes had her hands placed on her boyfriend's middle back. Gradually, that desire to touch became an indescribable magnetism that made them come together progressively towards their waists. With each kiss, he pulled her back towards him until her hips were hugging his groin, sitting on top of him. The scene was quite scandalous for a couple falling in love in the year 1950, although the reality was that there was not a soul in the entire vicinity capable of discovering them, hearing them or stopping them; they were completely alone. Dolores was enjoying the sinful thrill of sitting on Samuel's lap, with her legs around his waist, pushing gently toward him. Sgt. Pérez's hands had already gone far enough down and were inside her dress and squeezing the back of her thighs. Sitting on the swing, that urge to rock on each other grew and, slowly but progressively, their bodies began to produce friction between their groins. They both felt that enormous pressure in their sexes that flirted with discovering that furtive pleasure, forbidden in those times before marriage. They felt like outlaws, guilty of a crime they did not believe should be punished by others. Then, in a more accelerated way, they uncovered themselves from the waist up. It was dark, but he could still see her breasts, feel her lips and hear her heartbeat. Once lust took over the moment, there was no guilt in that act, only love. Their hands moved over each other's skin and their lips savored, between saliva, breath, sighs and gasps, the perfect taste of fornication. Samuel caressed Dolores' nipples with his lips and she enjoyed Samuel's incessant rubbing of her crotch. They were both virgins and inexperienced, which is why they did not understand the urge to rub against each other. Unrestrained, their sighs became audible as they exchanged sweat, kisses, tremors and uncontrollable sexual fury. After forty-one minutes of clothed fornication, they both felt an internal explosion, followed by a slow trembling that subsided with each pulse of their arousal. Once they finished, they lay stiffly on the swing, carrying in their bodies a very strong smell of sex that neither of them had ever smelled before. That night they had just made love without penetration.

The next morning they felt a little embarrassed because of the rush of desire they had experienced during the previous night, but, after a couple of minutes of silence, they became acclimated to the idea that it was perhaps an occurrence that would not be repeated. Self-consciously, they talked about everything except the event, as if it had never really happened. Despite the loud silence between the two, it didn't take long for them to repeat it. After three days of complete shattering abstinence, they synchronized the same scene of that first night. Even though they continued the custom of meeting twice a day, they now did so with different motives. During the daylight hours they would talk and share poetry or laugh about anything. In the evenings, they would wrap themselves around each other, and slowly the lustful rubbing became more direct, until their bodily fluids were daily on each other's skins, as they loved each other half-naked. Although there was never direct copulation, it was clear that their desires and virginities were exclusive to each other.

Everything continued to happen in the same fashion until, on a Friday, August 25, 1950, Sgt. Pérez was called to leave for that ill-fated date in Korea. The deployment orders shocked everyone in his company, creating a huge organizational mess and a dismal mood around the soldiers. Immediately after the news reached him, Samuel arranged various matters within the camp and rushed to Dolores' house. Upon arrival, he was wearing his military uniform and carried a pale look under his eyes. In his right hand he held a handwritten letter without an envelope, folded four times with the name "Dolores Fuertes" written on it. As coherently as he could, he told her in detail the specifics of what was about to happen. He did not know much about the exact locations but he knew Korea was farther than he had ever been in his life. In addition, he explained that this might be the last time they saw each other but that he would do everything under his power to survive this deployment, promising her to marry her when he returned. He then handed her the letter and asked her not to read it until he left. That night they stayed together until 4:43 a.m., at which time he had to meet his fellow soldiers and get on the bus that would take them to San Juan, starting their journey to the Korean War. Dolores and Samuel said goodbye with their hearts in their hands and tears rolling down their cheeks. During that sad Saturday morning, they vowed eternal love to each other, no matter what, and kissed with all the love each could express. At 5:30 a.m., Sgt. Samuel L. Pérez's battalion marched off to war.

∬Ninth

The day was sunny. Not at all the kind of Saturday Ian liked to have. He got up and made coffee, two pieces of toast and a fried egg. He ate very slowly, but with trepidation about having to take a shower. Once he had washed the dishes, he ventured into the bathroom with a little *aquaphobia*. He turned on the shower and there it was, the squirt. This time he wasn't going to try to tease him but let him have all his tantrums. Yes, he would let *Mr. Squirt* get cranky from his heat. He took a cold bath in less than a minute and a half. As soon as he finished washing, he turned off the faucet and jumped out of the tub.

Ian Samuel began work on a new condominium building project on the corner of Concordia and Mendez-Vigo streets. He drew lines on top of the blueprint, used a T-square to draw the angles, then programmed into his computer an exact simulation of the structure, calculated the strength of the foundation, the moment of its forces, the width of the columns, the rigidity of that material, the amount of pressure it could withstand, the width of the pipes, the passage of electricity; he made sure he had designed a safe building. At 1:03 p.m. he heard a knock on his apartment door. His bruises were still sore, so he walked slowly to the entrance.

"Hello, neighbor!" Ian heard as he opened the door. It's been about two weeks since I've seen you anywhere," said the man in an old-fashioned Spanish accent.

"I've been busy," Ian replied.

"Man, you have to pace yourself, otherwise you'll never grow old."

Ian was well aware of the great age his neighbor was referring to, as Don Ponce de León had to have been about 550 years old, give or take, judging by his clothes and appearance. This gentleman was six feet tall, had a rather long, wrinkled nose, and his face was white, with pink marks on his cheeks that were probably caused by an untreated case of *rosacea*. This Spanish man was old-fashioned. He sported a musketeer's mustache that trailed from his nose to the sides of his nose in concentric spirals and wore an armor that looked as if it had been cast in colonial times. The breastplate was bathed in something that was once silver and today looked like rust with traces of *tetanus*. He also carried in his right hand a small sword, which was also rusty, that gave signs of not having been useful for a long time. His full name was Don Juan Ponce de León. According to him, he had returned to Puerto Rico swimming from Hispaniola, after having failed his conquest for youth in Florida, the land of swamps and oranges. Truthfully, he was extremely obnoxious. He would talk for hours, as he boasted that this island was absolutely nothing until he had set foot on it, to govern it, many hundreds of years before. He then would double down on his insolence by talking about how he was the one who brought to Borinquen progress, religion and civilization as God, the Virgin Mary and the Catholic Monarchs commanded. Of course, he never touched on the fact that he also helped to kill thousands of Taínos, the native indigenous people of the Caribbean and Puerto Rico, as he made them their slaves, searching for gold and raping their women. However, despite his age, the old man always made sure no one would dare to fight him, for he spoke of expeditions that have never been read about, supposedly, because he would kill the chronicler before he could tell what happened and thus steal the scoop. With this in mind, Ian Samuel never dared to contradict anything he said, since he did not want to experience the reddish-brown of that moldy, tetanus-toting little sword.

Don Juan lived in the apartment #011b, to the left of Ian's, while the apartment on the right, #001b, was occupied by another old man who was somewhat younger than the old Iberian. This other neighbor, who was a compatriot of the Engr. Pérez-Fuertes, spoke in an extremely articulate manner, with such conviction that he was almost capable of making even a rock meditate.

The neighbor in #001b's name was simply Don Eugenio. For some reason, he never revealed his last name. Even if Ian knew nothing about his friend's lineage, he preferred the old man from #001b because he was simpler than his ancient counterpart from #011b and, really he was neither aggressive nor offensive. Eugenio never threatened anyone with moldy swords, but would use his intellect to talk sense into others. He was also taller than average, close to six feet in height. He had an ashen gray mustache that blended in with his groomed beard and physical image. His hair was the same grayish color as his mustache and he wore, close to his forehead, the incipient receding hairline of a baldness that most men suffer at his age. His gaze was very influential, his eyelids looked like some kind of electronic device, capable of penetrating your thoughts. As a result, without the need for words, he was very influential. His physical strength was quite impressive too, especially for a man of approximately 170 years of age, although this physical appearance was somewhat overshadowed by the five and a half centuries that Don Juan carried.

Although his stories had no swords, genocide of indigenous people or fountains of youth, Don Eugenio's tales were more interesting than those of Ian's neighbor to the left. He normally told, in a very succinct manner, the details of everything he had done and accomplished, which was quite impressive. One time he said that he wrote over forty books and numerous essays. On another occasion he told how he managed to build the first train in Argentina. If he had all the time in the universe, Ian would have spent much of it listening repeatedly to the many stories he loved so much about his favorite neighbor's experiences since they always made him feel good. From time to time, Eugenio would talk about his travels around the American continent, of the Chinese people he helped to free from their enslaved exploitation, of the many women he aided to gain civil rights around our sister countries, of the *Bayoán Pilgrimage,* of his many efforts to improve the most important part of any culture, its education, and of how he refused to be buried in his beloved island until it was liberated from colonialism. Above all these stories was a phrase that he continued to repeat day and night, rain or shine: "I only hope that people will one day say: on that island (Puerto Rico) was born a man who loved the truth, wanted justice and worked for the good of humanity." In short, his anecdotes were totally real, unlike the truthful fragments mixed with fiction narrated by Don Juan. In addition, his words carried a profound, almost philosophical message.

Don Ponce de León had arrived that day to make sure that Ian was alive, although he decided to stay and chat for a while. Five minutes after the worn-out colonist had arrived in Ian's room, Don Eugenio's cane was heard knocking on the door.

"Good afternoon, dear neighbor," said Don Eugenio in a slow and precise manner, "I came because I could not resist the desire to talk with such an odd couple of intellectuals as yourselves."

"Well, come in and settle down, sir, I was about to tell the story of the colonization of your country again," shouted Don Juan with his little sword raised high.

Ian looked at Don Eugenio with an apologetic expression mixed with embarrassment. The latter hated the whole story of tyranny and massacre that he had heard on numerous occasions from the lips of Don Juan Ponce de León. But, as Don Eugenio was a gentleman and had already had numerous arguments with him on the subject, he preferred to ignore the Spanish colonizer's bad manners and sat down in his appointed chair.

"Hey, you guys don't say hello anymore," said Ernie in an annoyed tone. "They come in here, sit down and treat me like the rest of humanity, like a lamp."

The trio smiled and looked up at him.

"*Mi amigo duende,*" replied Don Eugenio merrily, referring to him being his elf friend, "it is always a pleasure to have your cheerful and joyful presence."

"Mr. Ernie, if you want, I'll bring you here so you can join my colonial victory story," said Don Juan as he looked at Don Eugenio defiantly.

"No, that's not necessary, I've heard enough of that story, I'd rather sleep," retorted Ernie.

In fact, all those present, with the exception of Don Juan, preferred to sleep rather than listen to his boring fake legends. Either way, the Spaniard began telling his dull story that lasted for almost two hours. When he finished, he waved and blew kisses to the audience as if it had been a theatrical play, while wiping several tears from his cheeks. Once his poor performance was over, Ian took it upon himself to say goodbye to his two visitors and then lay down on his bed.

"Are you feeling all right?" Daly asked lovingly, "You look tired."

"I know, it's just that I have several things in my head and I hate, detest, loathe the damned colonial history of Puerto Rico that is repetitively brought up by Don Ponce de León."

"Honey, rest and you'll see how everything will go away," whispered Dalymar, leaning on his right arm.

"My love, what I feel is not going to disappear after I rest, not now, not ever," said Ian, ready to begin a monologue that he was tired of repeating. "Daly, look at me. The most important part of my universe is you and I have no way to share you with others. There is no way to talk to our families, no way to have a cup of tea while chatting in the corner café. If people hear us talking, they'll think I'm crazy and try to push you away and put me in an asylum. But am I really crazy, am I wrong for seeing "fantasies" that are invisible to their eyes, or are they wrong for using their senses to judge me? I am aware of my reality. I am fully conscious that I am somewhat unique for clinging to you, for not letting you leave my life, because you make up my world, my heaven, my everything. I know I am different for sharing with Ernie, a lamp in the shape of an elf, and treating him like a little brother. I also know that it is not normal to talk to Don Juan and Don Eugenio, knowing that no one else, besides us, sees them. But am I really crazy? I work day by day, I contribute to society with my knowledge, I pay my debts and my taxes, I have never failed in that. However, I prefer to live in my world and to move away from the one that becomes crueler every day. Why can't I cling to what I know as life? Why should I return to a place where the only things that matter are money, weapons and the imaginary power they provide? But what do I know? I, apparently, am totally unbalanced! That's probably why I don't understand why a nation like Iraq, which cried out in vain for help not to be invaded, should be slaughtered. But what do I know? I, apparently, am totally unbalanced! Perhaps because of this I do not understand the monetary waste of nations on biological weapons and nuclear bombs when really if they wanted to end the injustices of the world that money should be invested in ending hunger, in educating the masses or in any other pacifist purpose. Real solutions, we need real solutions. But what do I know? I, apparently, am totally unbalanced! Maybe if I were sane, I could understand a lot of things. I would know more about why people prefer to destroy themselves with debt and only care about maintaining an image before society that paints a fictitious portrait other than the one which they have been dealt. Possibly, if it were not for my madness, I could quench my thirst to understand what motivates a "rational" human being to abandon their parents as they age. How can there be so many wandering old people, adrift from that destiny they never imagined they would inhabit, much less after having dedicated themselves with great determination to raise their children, who ended up becoming crows that gouged out their eyes? But what do I know? I, apparently, am totally unbalanced! Maybe that's why they haven't jailed the man who caused your death, even though it was he who ran a red light and broke the law while blowing "just under the limit" for, regardless of the millions of technicalities his lawyers managed to come up with, along with their application of the "rational" laws that govern them. But what do I know? I, apparently, am totally unbalanced!

Once he finished speaking, his face was so red that it looked like he was about to suffer a massive myocardial infarction or a stroke. His breathing was no longer slow, but short and agitated, while his eyes were somewhat teary, more out of anger than sadness. Dalymar was hugging him, leaning on his neck, silently trying to calm him. From the day he met Ernie, Ian realized he was different from everyone else. Deep inside, he was always aware that his unbalanced world was a better one than the one in which the rest of humanity preferred to live; even though, in everyone's eyes, his reality belonged to a totally deranged man.

∬Tenth

The name of their regiment was the 65th Infantry. Samuel and almost all the members of the 65th were Puerto Ricans, under the age of twenty-five, and (with very few exceptions) totally unaware of why they were there. Once the ship docked in Korea, everyone was astonished when they could not find any stars in the sky. The night was dark, quiet and it looked as if they were walking straight into the mouth of the enemy. It was as if the moon and the clouds were trying to hide the sadness of that immense and inaudible emptiness they were about to unleash. For many of those men who had just disembarked, it was the first week in which they did not hear the singing of the coquí frogs in the distance or smell the strong odor of chicken manure from the mountain. On Korean soil, Samuel felt helpless, nauseated and sad.

The first night was short but quiet and, once the sun fell onto his eyes, Sgt. Samuel Luis Pérez found no substantial difference between that geography and the one of his Puerto Rico. The landscape was composed of mountains lined with green trees, full of mosquitoes and insects. The trees were nested with rambunctious birds and the loud rivers filled the immensity of the jungle with life. But the taste of the wind was different, the breeze did not cheer him as it did in his homeland and the humidity was not as passionate as it was in his beloved Borinquen.

None of those who made it to that war knew it, but the moment they put their boots on the ground, each was included on an invisible and exact list that no one would ever read or know about, but that would dictate their fates. In essence, the dice were already cast. On the list, the names of all the members of the regiment were written in different colors and, depending on the dye, it was how they were to depart from that Korean War.

For example, the name of eighteen-year-old José Martínez, originally from Salinas, PR, was written in *red* and, unbeknownst to him, he would die in the middle of an attack on a North Korean battlefield and his body would never be found. If the names were written in *gray*, then they would arrive back in PR, but locked in a coffin, cold from head to toe, as dead as José Martínez, but buried on the island where they were born. On the other hand, those whose names were written in *blue* were fated to return home without some piece of their body, be it feet, hands or any other part of their anatomy. Finally, there were those whose names were written in *gold*; they would return with their bodies fully intact, but with psychological damage and on the verge of delirium at some point in their lives. At the end of the conflict there was not a single name left of the members of the 65th Infantry that had not been included in that invisible list. In one way or another, everyone died a little, either in body or soul, in Korea. Although, in time, a few in *blue* or *gold* did recover enough to continue their lives.

It was on the battlefield, during the winter in Korea, that Samuel, for the first time, touched snow. They had been there a little more than three long months when, as they marched in a column, it began to snow before his very eyes and he smiled as he felt the wet frost melt between his fingers. His excitement was so great that all he wanted to do was to stop and write to Doly to tell her about it. Certainly, as he embarked for the war, he never imagined he would get his wish to see a snowstorm. Samuel never forgot that day for the rest of his life.

Despite the great initial sensation of the sudden appearance of snow, the reality was that his regiment was not trained to fight against the white enemy that so besieged them. In fact, most of the soldiers had never been exposed to such conditions and, even worse, none of them were used to spending long hours in the cold. For the first few months, they were able to survive by using every piece of clothing they had to keep warm during their patrols, but their hands would freeze and their feet could not stand the pain every time they went out on duty. During those impenetrable nights there was no cure other than a good fire and four brick walls to shelter them, but they lodged in huts and many times it was impossible to build a fire for fear of being discovered.

As in all wars, there is always a subjective good guy and a subjective bad guy. In this case the communists, those in the North Korean military, were the obvious subjective bad guys. The North Koreans had led millions of attacks against humanity and democracy. For this reason, the alliance between the President of the United States of America and the leader of South Korea turned American soldiers into heifers grazing among North Korean jungles and lethal traps. The 65th, along with many other American regiments, were in charge of making that alliance a reality. Their orders were to try to stop the communists and punish them, even though almost none of them even knew how to find Korea on the world map. Those soldiers were young, strong and very dedicated. They certainly loved their homeland and were willing to fight for freedom. There was not one of them who loved war, but they still fought the war like heroes.

During that terrifying winter, the Northerners used all their might to, along with the snow, freeze the 65th Infantry. The Puerto Ricans had to fight tooth and nail to avoid succumbing completely to the bullets and the cold, but, in the end, they were able to hold them off.

Samuel could never forget that first winter attack in Korea. It was about 10:54 a.m. when the ground and sky shook as they felt a shell strike the earth. Then a hail of explosions surrounded them, scattering snow and turning it into a black slush with fire, smoke and thunder that smelled like death. For about ten minutes they felt adrift in a sea of screams, amid waves of blood, senseless gunfire and confusion. Right after the first shell, Samuel had fallen to the ground, as if trying to become invisible. After several seconds, he pulled out his rifle and began to shoot wherever he could in front of him. He was shaking in fear, his heart beat faster than his shots and he felt as if the only thing his brain could see were mountains of snow filled with tidal waves of fire, ashes and bullets. Samuel could not stand it any longer, at that very moment he began to retreat and started to give orders for them to follow him.

"Fall back, fall back!" he shouted.

At that point, at least twenty-five soldiers were in a totally indistinguishable tangle of limbs. Their names had just been written in *red* within the list. Still, he reaffirmed his order. Thankfully, as they fled in disarray without much hope, they started to hear their own fighter aircrafts flying overhead. Their bombers came to the rescue and managed mitigate the enemy's shells and grenades that had been raining down from above. For the first time that morning, they felt some relief. However, the 65th continued to run for about two extra hours, until they reached the barricades again. That morning more than twenty-five souls would never return to Puerto Rico.

The Borinqueneers, as they started calling themselves after that first winter attack, were truly resilient. Despite the casualties recorded in that battle, they did not lose many more soldiers during the rest of the wintertime. They tried every trick they could think of in order to survive; from sleeping against each other on their backs to not sleeping for thirty-six hours at a stretch. But the more attacks they survived, the more time they spent tolerating that polar cold. Predictably, the North Koreans knew that, once sick, they would be weaker and more susceptible, so it was just a matter of waiting for the right moment before resuming their attacks. One of the first Puerto Ricans to become ill, both in body and spirit, was Sgt. Pérez.

During those times, Samuel had acquired the habit of taking advantage of his few free moments to write to his beloved Dolores. In his letters, he tried to tell her about everything, from the white and cold of the snow to every detail of the constant fear in which he lived. Day by day, he feared he would die. The truth was, if it hadn't been for the existence of Ms. Fuertes or those letters he so loved to write, Samuel might never have lasted much longer than a couple of weeks in Korea. It was that illusion of someday seeing her again that helped him do everything he could to try to survive. It was as if every smile, every kiss on the swings behind Dolores' house and every moment together had saved his life. In his mind, he loved her purely.

In the ranks of the North's communist army there was a surname, Kao, which belonged to a certain Hidoki. Hidoki was a soldier who had just joined the North Korean army less than a year before. Mr. Kao believed in water, in the sun and in that prodigious photo that reminded him of his fiancée, Jin Lukata. But this was not the only thing Hidoki believed in. He also believed in electricity, in the injustices of the South's army, in the innocence of children and in the death of his father at the hands of the Americans.

One night in mid-spring, Samuel woke up with an urge to urinate. Because a war zone is not the safest place to go out to use the bathroom in the middle of the night, Samuel hefted his rifle in his left hand and walked out into the night's darkness. Once outside his hut, he looked to his left and noticed that Ramón Celestino, who was on watch, was still surprisingly awake. He then walked to the nearest bushes, placed his rifle on the ground and proceeded to irrigate the surrounding bushes. Samuel was so intent on the act that he did not initially notice the presence of a dark shadow behind him.

"Click!" Sgt. Pérez heard over his right ear. He dissimulated for the space of 5.13 seconds as he pondered why the hell he had dropped his rifle. After mentally recreating his next moves, he looked slyly at the ground and caught, with his right eye, part of the shadow of a pointy hat standing behind him. The shadow was somewhat deformed by the ravages of the night, but it was accurate enough to reveal that it belonged to the enemy, the Communists. Once he was sure that it was not an ally, Samuel turned toward the figure. As he twisted, Sgt. Pérez pressed his military knife in the direction of the enemy shadow that had been sniffing him. But, even as he tried his best to press his tactical scalpel, the shadow made a sudden movement with his right hand that managed to hit him in the forehead and knock him onto his back. That sudden strike, rendered him unconscious. Sgt. Pérez found himself compromised, with his back planted on the ground.

When he opened his eyes, he felt a gigantic headache and his vision was a little blurry. After several seconds, he began to sharpen his gaze and realized that he was not alone. Hidoki Kao was standing right in front of him. Samuel didn't hear him speak much during the first few minutes of his capture. Mr. Kao had been sent by his company to spy on the 65th and, just as he was positioning himself in the bushes, Samuel arrived, with death in hand and a sharp, annihilating knife. Now, lying on the ground,

Samuel was tied by a piece of rope that made it impossible for him to move his hands. As he looked at his captor, he perceived a young man between twenty and twenty-five years of age with a fair complexion and smaller than average height. Hidoki had dark brown eyes and spiky, jet-black hair. The young man was dressed in white, with a black belt around his waist and a conical straw hat on his head. Unfortunately, Sgt. Pérez knew he was not lying on the ground for recreational purposes. He estimated that he was a prisoner of war and, at the very least, he would be tortured for several months or, much more likely, executed.

It was at 00:17 hours when he and Kao met on that starry night. By the time his companions found him, Samuel and the North Korean had had enough of listening to each other.

"What is your name?" asked Hidoki in perfect Spanish.

Samuel looked around, closed his eyes and banged his head against a tree, knowing that it was impossible for an Asian member of the enemy forces to speak Spanish with a Puerto Rican accent. For this reason, he remained mute until he heard the same voice again.

"Do you have a name or are you mute?" asked the enemy soldier sarcastically.

"I have a name, but what do you care?" Samuel replied defiantly. "What the hell do you want to know for? Just kill me and end your stupid games."

Hidoki Kao burst out laughing so loudly that Samuel was surprised it was not heard by anyone.

"Just kill me? Ha! Are you blind, crazy or what? Haven't you noticed that I'm the one who's dead here?"

Indeed, Hidoki was absolutely right. Looking again, Samuel was stiffened, so much so that he felt as if his being was immobilized by some Korean invisible witchery. Sgt. Pérez thought himself a fool for not having noticed that, in effect, his military knife, all seven inches of it, was stuck in the center of his dead chatterbox's chest.

"But, if you're dead, how the hell can you talk to me and look at me like that? Why can't I undo these knots and run away from here?"

Samuel waited for the obvious answer, until he heard it from the lips of someone else; somebody who didn't really exist anymore.

"Elementary, my dear victimizer. I am dead in life, but not in existence. Even though you ended a part of me, I will forever remain by your side. The bonds you see in your hands do not exist, the lips you watch move are mute, and the only reason you think you are imprisoned is because of your conscience."

Samuel reflected for several minutes and realized that this explanation made more sense than any other that could clarify the event. Hidoki Kao, the dead man who was talking to him, was the fruit of his mind, the effect of his conscience. From that night until the moment in which Samuel's life expired, Hidoki Kao stayed by his side to remind him of the fateful event. After those tense moments filled with rage and traumatic guilt, they both relaxed and tried to become acquainted with each other. As a result, under the light of the Korean sky, they both learned each other's names and talked about their families, their positions in the military and how much they hated the war. They spent perhaps a little over five hours conversing without any interruption, as if the night had been reserved for them to become friends.

When they finally located Sgt. Pérez, they found him shivering from the cold and with a fever so high that he was capable of warming the entire platoon. By then, between months of not eating very well, staying awake for long hours and with poor hygiene, he had caught a few viral respiratory infections. The last one had been a flu, which was complicated by a superimposed bacterial pneumonia. With every second, that lung infection threatened to turn into a progressive and fulminant sepsis. Without antibiotics, he was merciless against those killer bacteria, affectionately known as *pneumococcus*. As a result, Samuel spent two nights in full delirium, babbling and coughing up a very thick, painful phlegm, mixed with blood, sweat and pus. At that time there were not many antibiotics around the world and, in wartime, there were only enough to treat those who had the best chance of surviving, so his only hope was to fight this infection until he could reach the infirmary ship that was a little less than three days from his location. On the way to the ship, he spent two long and painful nights, lying on the ground praying frantically that he would not die. In reality, the probability that he would survive was slim and, in his case, hope and prayers were all he had left.

To the great fortune of his offspring, Samuel did make it to the hospital ship. Once he was given sufficient penicillin, IV fluids and gradually cured of the ravages of his pneumonia, Sgt. Pérez was placed back in action. Luckily for him, he did not return alone to the battlefield, though. As promised on his death-bed, Hidoki stayed present in all his battles, he also witnessed every love letter he sent to Dolores from the Asian terrain and became, really, the only friend he had during his time in Korea. Mr. Kao turned out to be his faithful companion on night watches, the minimal comfort on anxious afternoons, and his rear vision in enemy ambushes. In essence, Hidoki Kao was the reason Samuel's name was written in *gold* and not *red* or *black* on the invisible list of the 65th Infantry.

Before leaving the Korean War, Samuel vowed never to forget the bitter winter nights along the *Hangang River*, the green meadows he walked through during spring, the many flowers he saw blossom and the immensity of nature in that suffering nation. The truth was that, upon his return, Samuel could only remember the millions of innocent people who witnessed the fury of his explosive armament; the poor children, who saw their dreams disintegrate and turn into death; the families who experienced, in their own flesh, how a cloud of pain covered the death of their loved ones. But, above all, Sgt. Samuel Luis Pérez would never forget how lucky he was to return to Puerto Rico more alive than dead, even though his name was ultimately written in *gold*. Sadly, Samuel traded his reason to keep his breath and honor his country.

∫∫Eleventh

When she opened her eyes, Dolores Fuertes felt a huge shiver that ran through every vertebra of her back and twisted every axon of her spinal cord. Silently, she was afraid to know the meaning of that premonition; she had the feeling that something sinister was about to happen. Indeed, on the day she felt that flow of electrons through her back, Samuel had the joy of meeting Hidoki Kao. In spite of this, neither Dolores, nor anyone else in this universe, would ever know this detail, since it would be a secret that Sgt. Pérez would take to his grave.

After waking up, Doly buttoned up her skirt and her blouse, then placed the halter around her neck that held her white apron. Once dressed, she headed to the bathroom, where she brushed her teeth, removed some rheum from her eyes and used her mother's hairbrush to fix her disheveled hair. Afterwards, she brewed a strong, dark coffee, which she served in a cup but didn't finish completely, leaving some for her younger sister, who was still asleep. Lastly, she headed out the back door and straight to the street.

Both of Dolores' parents were pharmacists, which is why they had set up a small apothecary on the edge of the central mountain range of Puerto Rico. For the longest time, everyone in her family was very happy, but the death of her father, Mr. Ramón Fuertes, turned Dolores' mother, Mrs. Gisela Fuertes, into a social alcoholic. Thus, slowly, the Fuertes family's life turned into a nightmare. It all started with a missed diagnosis of *leptospirosis* that took the life of Doly's father. Had he had received a single dose of penicillin, perhaps Dolores' story and, for that matter, the saga of her whole family, would have been quite different. As a result, without the correct treatment, Ramón died of fulminant liver and multiorgan failure, *jaundiced* from head to toe and in complete agony. He suffered every second of his accelerated death.

Now, three months after Mr. Fuertes' death, Doly had assumed the responsibility of taking over the pharmacy business. While her father was still alive, she used to help him with errands and other minor things, from 3 p.m. to 5 p.m., but she had never been in sole responsibility of the day-to-day decisions. However, since she had recently finished her high school studies and her family needed her, she decided to skip college and attend the store as a full-time job, from 7 a.m. to 3 p.m. The plan was originally to do it with the help of her mom, Gisela, but she quickly became an absent pharmacist and mother after her husband's departure. Unfortunately, her younger sister, Rosita, was four years younger than her and still too young to help run the drug store.

During those days, Dolores' life would iterate around the same endless and boring routine. First, she would get ready and make coffee, say goodbye to Rosita and then go out the back. She would later arrive to open the doors of the *Fuertes Pharmacy*, located near the outskirts of town, and wait for the clientele. Once there, she normally had to listen, at list once per day, to Dr. Evaristo and scorn his indecent proposals, then sweep the lonely entrance and mop the floor tiles. During lunchtime, she would look at the pictures of her beloved Samuel and remember how much she loved him, read the folded letter he gave her right before departing, smell the loneliness in the air and weep tears of sadness. Then she would turn on the radio and pray for the end of the war, which had plunged her dreams into anguish, while waiting hopefully for the mailman to deliver a letter from her boyfriend. Again and again, this sequence of painful, sad, and cyclical steps was repeated; certainly, the monotony of their recurrence was one of the first contributors to the future transformation of Ms. Fuertes into Doña Mother.

It was during a mid-December afternoon, when Dolores received her first love letter from Samuel. As soon as the envelope was handed to her, she felt a thick mixture of relief and joy spreading through her skin; indeed, she was ecstatic. She devoured each sheet of the letter so quickly that, when she finished reading the last line, she searched through the mailbox hoping to find another one, but found nothing. As a result, she reread the letter over and over again, until she had almost memorized every line within the message of love written by him. In a matter of hours, she became so immersed within the confines of Sgt. Pérez's stories that she could live every bullet that was fired on North Korean soil, she could glimpse every life erased from the futile list of the 65th Infantry, and she could breathe in every ounce of exhaustion that the letter sheltered.

Although Samuel wrote approximately eighty-nine love letters to Dolores, he never mentioned Hidoki Kao or his *pneumococcal* pneumonia. Each letter contained his anecdotes over the past seven days. They always began and ended in the same way. First, he would tell her, in great detail, what he had done during the day, his fears, the battles and the awfulness of the war. Then he would tell her for several paragraphs how much he loved her and that tomorrow… Yes, with the word "tomorrow", he would close the body of his daily anecdote and leave open the beginning for the next day. Finally, on the last day of the week, he would say goodbye, repeat that he loved her and continue with the Puerto Rican version of *One Thousand and One Nights* from Korea.

Dolores remained in charge of the *Fuertes Pharmacy* throughout the depression caused by the war. At the age of nineteen, she had to pull herself up by her bootstraps to keep her family afloat, either by working tirelessly or by eating less and less to concentrate on the daily tasks. As time went by, the only hope she had of any salvation was encapsulated in the future arrival of Samuel from the Asian mountain ranges. In the solitude of the family drugstore, she learned to hide her feelings of joy and began, gradually, to accelerate her process of hatred towards humanity. In general, there were days that passed more quickly, but those that did not, those that were stationary, seemed to be perpetual in her mind.

Even when her mother, Gisela, was still alive, she was completely useless. At forty-five years of age, she still retained a good figure and her face looked the same as the once young and delicate woman who fell in love during college with her future husband, Ramón Fuertes. Unfortunately, with the death of Doly's father, her mother had acquired an increasingly progressive habit of dressing flirtatiously, wearing perfume, makeup and drinking exorbitant amounts of alcohol. At first, she did this out of depression, to escape her sorrows, but then she became convinced that perhaps she could find herself a new husband and return to her happiness. Six months after the event, the former Mrs. Fuertes was totally alone, and completely alcoholic. She drank so much that she slowly stopped eating and simply based her caloric intake in booze plus the occasional piece of fruit or slice of bread. She would be seen at *Cantina de Don Pedro* late into the night, accepting drinks from any man with enough money to pay for them. She was not poor, but she believed at the time this practice would help her find a new lover. Many times, they would give her these drinks for free, other times they would exchange them for a kiss or sexual favors. Soon, Mrs.

Gisela Fuertes, the only pharmacist in town, became the "scarlet woman" of the neighborhood, the *puta* and nightly courtship of many married men. As a result, the number of customers at the pharmacy, especially women, dwindled to the point that only people who had a very sick family member and no way to get to the next town or to San Juan were seen there.

Gradually, Dolores' world began to crumble until there seemed to be no escape. On countless occasions, she considered running away from it all to seek her luck somewhere else. She thought of everything, from becoming addicted to alcohol, like her mother, to slitting her wrists or ingesting one of the thousands of medicines they had at the back of the drugstore in order to take her own life. Fortunately, her depression did not overcome her and she never attempted suicide; not for lack of desire, but because of the hope that Samuel one day would come back.

For this reason, the letters from Sgt. Pérez became the only joy she had in her life. Once the mailman delivered them, she knew two things: first, that at least several months ago, her beloved was alive and, second, that there was still hope that her dream would come true. Those letters were like a love from the past transported to the present, connecting her current self and the past self of Samuel, who wrote the letter three months earlier. Monthly, she received one, two and even three letters during the almost two years they were separated by the war. All signed with, "*I will love you forever, Samuel.*" All written with his love deeply carved into the written words.

Unfortunately, the day came when the joy of the correspondences turned into sadness. For a whole month, she did not receive a single letter written by Sgt. Pérez. And that sorrow would not end quickly, as one month turned into two months and, slowly, the days connected until the calendar marked five months without any news from her boyfriend. Dolores was tired, worried by the lack of communication over his status. Certainly, she lived in constant expectation of what may or may not have happened to him. Despite her best wishes, with time, the waiting only grew longer and longer and piled up like a mountain of dates marked by the fear of losing him. On a daily basis, her hopes were shattered by the uncertainty of not hearing from him. As a result, anxiety began to take over Dolores' soul.

During those days her only consolation was not receiving a telegram from the military announcing his death, but this ceased to calm her when she realized that they might never contact her, but would simply let his mother know, since they were not yet married. It was then that she began to search all the newspapers, to see if she could find him. She found nothing. She called the American Red Cross weekly, but no one could tell her anything. She tried to contact her future mother-in-law, whom she only knew the name but had never met, since she lived several towns away, but she was unsuccessful. Finally, she gave up any idea of happiness and began to withdraw into a state of complete alienation which, as the days went by, took on an impenetrable shade.

Depression quickly robbed her of hunger and sleep. She hardly ate anything or slept, she only drank water, black coffee and orange juice. She lost a lot of weight, almost thirty pounds, and at some point she looked so thin that her clothes barely fit her. She spent her nights staring at the ceiling, locked in her room and sweating from head to toe, watching the insects fly over the mosquito net of her bed. She had not spoken to Cecilia, her best friend, for months. In fact, in those days she opened the pharmacy at 12:00 p.m. and closed it at 2:45 p.m., when the mailman came by.

Mrs. Fuertes, for her part, continued to go from bad to worse. Due to the peculiar notoriety she had created around town, men not only waited for her to arrive at the *Cantina de Don Pedro*, but sometimes showed up at her house with bottles of rum and their willing penises, where they normally spent the whole night drunk and satisfied.

The Fuertes' house soon took on an almost brothel-like appearance; to such a degree that, at least once a week, on Fridays or Saturdays, scattered groups of three and four women would arrive and spend their evenings partying with men, smoking and drinking, inside the remaining four rooms of their once very Christian home. The visitors would enter in the company of unknown individuals and leave used, with the perfume of cigarettes, rum and beer all over their bodies. By then, Doly no longer cared what happened. For her, life was over; especially if her beloved was dead.

This alienation in which she was submerged came to an end during one of many nights when her mother once again turned the home where she grew up into a makeshift, clandestine brothel, while she was having one of her big parties. The moon was typical for mid-August, and the hands of the clock kissed at 11:55 p.m. She had just spent the evening at Cecilia's house, for the first time in over six months, crying and trying to clear her mind away from her pathetic present. When she arrived home, she found empty liquor bottles in the front yard. Then she opened the front door and was convinced that the smell of cigarettes, chlamydia and gonorrhea was no coincidence. Apparently, all the whores in the neighborhood were gathered there. But that night would be different, perhaps by fate or bad luck, because just before climbing the stairs, Dolores heard a familiar voice that stopped her heart. She hurriedly reached the upper floor of the house to discover her younger sister, Rosita, totally drunk, almost unconscious, and with her legs wrapped around an unknown man who was brusquely raping her, attempting to turn a kid into a woman. Dolores did not lose her temper for an instant. Instead, she walked briskly to the kitchen on the first floor, took out the family revolver from the main junk drawer, which her father had taught her to use, together with a box of bullets, and, once in hand, went up the stairs again, two by two, straight to her sister's room. As she stepped through the door, she began firing indiscriminately into the walls, ceiling and windows, while screaming, "get out of my house or I will kill you, *pricks*", which immediately led to the sound of accelerated footsteps that could be heard from every corner, rushing down the stairs and banging the doors as they left. Instinctively, Doly continued firing into the ceiling, reloading the revolver as she walked from room to room, until there were no drunken men (or amateur prostitutes) left inside her mother's brothel. Finally, she reloaded the six chambers in the gun for the third time and set about doing what she thought ought to have been done a long time ago.

With a sturdy step, Miss Fuertes walked straight to her mother's room, without even stopping to help her younger sister, who was lying on her bed, in a bath of liquor, blood and sweat. When she reached Mrs. Gisela Fuertes' bedroom, she found her lying on her bed, surrounded by garbage and damp semen patches.

"*Bitch*! Pick up your things or I swear I'll shoot you dead with Papi's gun. Then I'll cut you to pieces with a machete and bury them under some bush so the rats and cockroaches eat you for dinner," said Dolores with a conviction so great it was impossible to ignore.

"Papi? Daughter, what are you saying, Papi is dead, I'm trying to find another father for you and Rosita," she said in her rum and schnapps lingo.

Dolores wasted no more time. She simply raised the .22 caliber revolver to shoulder height and pulled the trigger. The shot passed one and a half inches to the right of her almost victim's head. In reality, she missed. Her real intention was definitely to kill her. After that ill-advised shot, her mother got out of bed with one hand to her right ear, screaming and trembling as she struggled to pack a small suitcase. She would never, ever, ever see her again or know her exact whereabouts. Her lawyers arranged to transfer everything to Doly's name, on the condition that she would not be taken to court for what she allowed to be done to Rosita that night. Embarrassed and without much choice, Gisela signed all the papers, withdrew the remainder funds she still had in the bank and left for good. Years later, Dolores heard rumors that she had eloped with one of her many lovers to New York, where she died alone, homeless, in a women's shelter almost three years after that night she had almost killed her. Frankly, Ms. Fuertes didn't care. Her metamorphosis into the future Doña Mother was almost complete.

It took her many months to do it but getting her mother out of her life was much more therapeutic than any antidepressant or antipsychotic medication. For several weeks she dedicated herself to taking care of Rosita, cleaning the house and fixing every detail that her mother had destroyed thanks to her alcoholism and, probably also, sex addiction. Her actions, and how she got Gisela Fuertes out of her life, were well appreciated by the whole town. Slowly, more customers began to use *Fuertes Pharmacy* and she was able to hire a full-time pharmacist to replace her mother (who ironically had not worked for a long time).

It was by the end of July, almost two years after Samuel had left for the war, that Dolores heard her doorbell ring in a rather peculiar way. Desperate to know if it was true, she ran outside until she reached the front door, where she saw the military man in uniform that she loved so much. To her surprise, Samuel was alive, although not as much as she thought. As soon as he saw her, he hugged her so tightly that Dolores felt as if he had never left for war.

"Will you marry me?" asked Samuel as soon as he finished hugging her.

"Yes, of course, yes! I love you, I love you, I love you, I love you!" replied Dolores, while she kissed him repeatedly and wiped her tears.

During that evening they made love to each other until late into the night, thus having the delight of what they had so long waited for. The next morning, Doly got up and cooked breakfast for her future husband. He sat down, ate every bite from the plate and returned to the room pretending that he was the same, that he had not changed. From that day on, their lives had been joined forever.

For all the love they felt for each other, their marriage was destined to be only a fragment of what it once had the potential to become. The truth was that, after Samuel's arrival from the war, neither of them were the same. They certainly loved each other, no doubt about it, and there was no one they would rather continue their lives with. But the young lovers of the past had gone, and they could never be the same again. They both looked at each other's faces and could not find the lips they had first kissed; nowadays, there were only the ravages of war, of depression, of guilt that had replaced those loving eyes and the sighs shared under the flamboyant tree. Samuel's killing of Hidoki Kao during the war had changed him, and Dolores had also changed by nearly shooting her mother. As a result, they made an unspoken pact to love each other in their own way and so grow old together.

It was the month after Samuel had arrived from Korea that they finally got married. The ceremony was Catholic and very small. Fewer than twenty people attended. A young version of

Father Rodrigo was the one who united them before God, in the capital, and they had a modest dinner in a private restaurant.

During the following week, Dolores left almost everything they inherited from their parents, including managing the *Fuertes Pharmacy*, to her younger sister. As time passed, they drifted apart but still tried to stay in touch. Unfortunately, Doly was never very close to her nephews, who were born before Sebastián and Ian. Nor did she pay much attention to her brother-in-law, Heriberto, who married Rosita and always treated her like a princess. Over the years, Rosita and Heriberto took over the pharmacy completely and she only saw them every other year, during some holiday occasion, or when the kids asked to spend some family time. Despite the lack of quality time, they always loved one another and called almost monthly to catch up. They also wrote letters and birthday cards, but they weren't really as close as they had once been. Perhaps it was a lack of motivation on both of their parts, but the truth is that Dolores always blamed herself for all the hurt her mother caused them; especially during that last night they saw her. Deep inside, she always felt ashamed that she had failed her little sister, even though it was not her fault.

After they were married, Mr. and Mrs. Pérez moved to a magnificent lake house, not far from San Juan, with hopes to forget their pasts. In that home they spent many long years together without conceiving children, until Mrs. Pérez finally became pregnant and soon changed her name. With great joy, Doña Mother gave birth to Ian Samuel, her firstborn, at the age of thirty-five.

∫∫Twelfth

When he arrived at his apartment, Sebastián still had Violeta's smile painted in his memory. After unbuttoning his shirt, he went to the bathroom and took a shower. Once finished, he wrapped himself in a robe and walked to the kitchen, ready for a quick dinner/snack. After a minute of careful deliberation, Seba went for a glass of red wine with Gouda cheese and crackers. As he cut the cheese into slices, images came to him of how strange that day had been. First, he remembered the heated arguments with his medical liability insurer, followed by that smell of woman mixed with blood at Ian's house while he tended to his injuries. Then he recalled the unwarranted visit from Doña Mother, along with the huge headache it caused him, leading to him almost fainting while driving. Lastly, he remembered the surprising presence of a beautiful stranger in front of his car, who he nearly killed by accident. Quietly, he drank some more wine as he thought to himself, "Yes, it was a rather bizarre day." Indeed, it was; even if he discounted that strange interaction with María, the deaf girl, who somehow knew Violeta's name. But, above all, the best part of the night had been the exquisiteness of Ms. Contreau's company while he drove her home.

Wine, crackers and cheese in hand, Seba walked into the living room, grabbed his remote control and pressed the red-oval button, with the letters "ANTENNA" written in white. Suddenly, images, more like memories, of his day began to appear. Sebastián had discovered this interesting capability of his television five years ago when he accidentally pressed the "ANTENNA" button instead of the "ON/OFF" button and had the opportunity to witness, in high-definition, the events he had experienced during that day.

Thanks to this informational extravaganza, Seba was able to replay or pause, in slow motion, rewind or fast forward, every moment he'd experienced while awake that day. Although it sounded extraordinary to have a device with these capabilities, he rarely used it. This was because it had several limitations. To remind himself of these, Sebastián had written them down on a cheat sheet with the empirical instructions he had compiled over its five years of use.

Rules for using the "ANTENNA" button:

1. To access its marvelous capabilities, you have to have the same genetic makeup and have been subjected to the same environmental and psychosocial pressures as Sebastián L. Pérez-Fuertes (thank God, it doesn't work with Doña Mother or anyone else but me).

2. You can only see the events that occurred during that day, in a first-person point of view, as late as ten minutes before pressing the button (or midnight, whatever comes first) and as early as 12:01 a.m. of that day (i.e., I cannot see anything older than 23 hours and 50 minutes or closer than ten minutes from when I started the TV).

3. It is impossible to record the images. If you try, you see static instead and you summon a deafening high-pitched

noise instead of the actual sound (believe me, I've tried it and, unfortunately, there is no way to save copies, you can only see it the day it happened).

4. Even if it was Sebastián L. Pérez-Fuertes who pressed the "ANTENNA" button, neither the images nor the sound can be enjoyed by anyone other than him (please refer to rule #1, no need to worry if I am not alone, no one else can snoop on me).

5. You can only see events that happened while you were awake. There is no way to gather information if you were not conscious (in other words, make sure you are alert, awake and oriented if you want to see something again, there is no way to rewatch what happened, was said or done to you while you were asleep, let alone if you did not see it).

6. If you are reading these instructions and you think, "Is Seba crazy?", you have fallen into my trap, this is a joke, enjoy my TV and repeat: "Viva Puerto Rico!"

With these five rules (and bullet number six, which served to scare off anyone snooping around his apartment and accidentally reading his empirical instructions), Sebastián was sure to use the "ANTENNA" button properly whenever he felt like it. For this reason, while driving to Violeta's house, he had tried to observe every detail about her. With the help of the television, he reviewed once again her eyes and the delicacy of her skin. He thought about how intense her gaze was and how lonely her goodbye was. Sebastián stayed glued to his TV until 11:59 p.m. and 59 seconds during that night; observing Violeta, studying her perfection. For some reason there was something about her that was different from the others. As soon as he turned off the device, he walked to his bedroom, changed into more comfortable clothes and went to bed.

When the alarm sounded, the clock read 9:12 a.m. For a second, he thought about staying in bed, but the frightening thought of missing his date with Violeta forced him to get up. For some reason, Seba felt the need to look to his right. As he did so, he found a note analogous to the first one, also written in black India ink and placed in the same position on his nightstand.

You have less than a year to live

Sebastián again felt the same fear, his heart pounded with desperation as he had the impression that his body was about to start levitating and perhaps flying straight to the Taj Mahal. However, this time he was able to control his emotions. Lying in bed, he thought about pressing the "ANTENNA" button and trying, unsuccessfully, to rewind a moment he did not observe while asleep, to perhaps capture the exact instant when that note had appeared. That quiet and cold note which apparently would remain present for the rest of this upcoming year. In reality, there was no point in looking for a culprit, especially with the use of his TV, since he remembered quite well bullet number five. "If I ever find the clown who wrote these notes, I'm going to give him an unforgettable beating," he thought to himself.

Even as his heart continued to pound, Sebastián decided to grab the note and, impulsively, he tore it to shreds and threw it in his wastebasket. Once he was sure he had destroyed it, he hurried his pace to get ready with the intention of forgetting, once again, what could perhaps be a notice of his final sentence.

His wristwatch read 10:47 a.m. when he arrived at his destination. The *Paseo de la Princesa*, in Old San Juan, looked as ideal as ever for a quiet stroll. Sebastián paused for a second to take in his surroundings with a deep sigh. Overhead, he could see the big blue sky and the brightness of the sun. The breeze was gentle, but refreshing and easy to breathe. A few children were running happily close to the nearby benches, jumping with joy and eating red slushies, probably raspberry flavored. Full of excitement, he continued walking quietly towards the end of the promenade until he reached the main fountain that was sculpted with intertwining silhouettes of men and women, as if forming some kind of victorious dance. While he contemplated the artistic figures, Sebastián thought once again about Violeta, who he had not been able to keep out of his mind since the previous night.

Thus, distracted by everything around him, Dr. Pérez-Fuertes did not, at first, notice the presence of his date in a corner of the walkway. She was sitting on a wooden bench inside a small interior garden. The minute he saw her, his heart did a flip. She was wearing a white dress and had a book on her lap which she was reading peacefully. He didn't know whether to say "hello" or remain silent. Deep inside, he felt the urge to watch her undisturbed as he tried to absorb every movement, keeping her in his memory. Without realizing it, a little more than five minutes passed before he decided to approach her and speak to her.

"Hello, what a coincidence to find you here this morning," said Seba finally.

"Who would have imagined," Violeta replied as her face instantaneously seemed a little flushed and she marked her page, closing her book.

"My name is Sebastián II, prince of these territories, and your name?"

"I am known as Princess Contreau, but most people call me Violeta," she replied, blushing slightly.

"Well, Princess Contreau, I would like to state that you have a beautiful smile."

"I thank thee for the compliment, but I regret to inform Your Highness that perhaps you have not seen enough Puerto Rican royal smiles around your kingdom," they both smiled.

Sebastián sat next to her and they talked for a little over two hours. Then they walked up the *Puerta de San Juan* and settled on a simple, *Criollo* restaurant for lunch. Violeta talked mostly about anecdotes from books, the Catholic Church and her brother Junior, the paralegal/writer. Sebastián told her about his parents, Ian and Doña Mama but very little about his work. The two remained glued to their conversation throughout the day until, at 7 p.m., they decided to walk around the rest of the touristy part of Old San Juan. They strolled along the docks and shared an ice cream, then walked up the cobblestone streets until they reached the *Castillo del Morro*. There, they sat on its green lawns and stargazed. As their time together increased that evening, their bodies began to smell each other's fragrance. Both Violeta and Sebastián knew that it was unusual the way they had met and that, if destiny existed, it surely had some purpose between them. It was not so easy to avoid that magnetic feeling that encouraged them to get closer and continue talking. It was at 12:15 a.m. when Violeta realized that she had long since exceeded her self-imposed curfew. But, unlike the day before, she refrained from saying anything.

"I am fascinated by your eyes," said Seba, as he gently stroked Violeta's hair.

"Thank you, but there's nothing special about them, they're normal," said Violeta, flirtatiously.

Just as Violeta stopped speaking, Seba slid his hands down her delicate neck. Slowly, their lips came closer until they kissed. They kissed for long hours, using each other as a refuge from the outside world, finding a way out from their ordinary lives into the sublime.

That night they stayed together until dawn. It had been fewer than three days since they met, but, despite the short period of time, during that early morning they both felt *that* which only with the soul is sensed. Truthfully, no matter how many sonnets or verses are written, even with all the prose of this universe, only by loving can one understand the true limits of sorrow and pleasure. Love is the train of our souls, which transports us to the happiest and saddest moments of life.

∬Thirteenth

Forty-seven dates distributed between dinners, boleros, salsas and cha-chas, walks on the beach, hikes in *El Yunque National Forest*, museums, galleries, wine tastings, movie theaters, ice cream, bookstores, novels, theater trips, concerts, libraries and, of course, church. All of these occurred little by little, once or twice a week, until they became routines, occurring on a daily basis.

Since that afternoon-evening-morning in Old San Juan, Sebastián and Violeta had shared forty-seven dates in seventy-two days. Miraculously, Dr. Pérez-Fuertes had acquired the fortunate habit of arriving early to his office, pleasantly attending to his patients and even giving them a smile as he went about his work. Instead of just three days, he was opening his office four days a week. On workdays he would arrive at 8 a.m. sharp, after picking Violeta up and taking her to work. He would then see half of his twenty to twenty-five patients before lunch. Right after finishing his lunch, he would go to the hospital to care for his inpatients and then return promptly to the operating room to do colonoscopies from 3 p.m. to 5 p.m., at which time he usually finished writing his notes and dictated his procedures. He would then chat for twenty minutes with Natalia as he helped her organize the medical files or balance the day's admissions and prepare to leave before 5:55 p.m. to pick up his girlfriend, Ms. Contreau.

Violeta, too, could feel the effects of her boyfriend. Certainly, there was something different in her eyes, a gleam of joy in her smile, a casual sigh of love. During a workday, she would now finish her work at 5:48 p.m., at which time she would punch her shift card, say goodbye to Víctor, the afternoon janitor, and walk to the corner of the library, where Seba usually parked. Monday through Friday this sequence occurred, regardless of whether Sebastián had the day off or not.

The seventy-second day, after they met, fell on a Friday and Violeta left at 5:59 p.m. through the main door of the municipal library of San Juan. Once she got into Sebastián's car, they greeted each other with a kiss, hugged for several seconds and exchanged proclamations of love.

"How was your day? asked Violeta as soon as she buckled her seat belt.

"It was very good, twenty-two patients and none of them, thank God, are in the intensive care unit. And you, Princess Contreau, how was your day?"

"Well, it was very good. Today several new editions of books arrived and I was quite entertained between a book on cardiac anatomy by Frank Netter and a collection of Puerto Rican short stories, called *La Anastomosis*, by Rafael Samuel García Cortés."

"Tremendous, both books sound very interesting, I'll have to read them. Hey, sorry to change the subject, but guess what I have in my right pocket," said Seba.

"Don't tell me, let me guess. Don't tell me..., let's see, you got two tickets to see the *New York Ballet* at the Fine Arts Center in San Juan."

Indeed, Sebastián had managed, after a month and a half of intense searching, to get two tickets to see the only performance at *El Centro de Bellas Artes de San Juan* of the *New York Ballet*, accompanied by the Puerto Rican Symphony Orchestra.

Although he was disappointed that he hadn't surprised her, Seba didn't feel bad. He knew, by instinct, that Violeta would guess; she almost always managed to anticipate his intentions.

"My love, I concede that you should know, in advance, every surprise I plan to give you. But please, at least tell me, how do you do it?" Seba begged with his eyes wide open.

"Honey, how many times have I told you that magicians don't reveal their tricks?" said Violeta as she winked at him.

They both smiled and continued talking about everything that had happened during the day. Though, of course, Seba only told the deed, not the doer: the health of his patients was confidential. After dropping Violeta off at her house, Sebastián went to his apartment, dressed appropriately, and looked into his bedroom wastebasket. It was filled with at least seventy-two discarded notes that foretold, in black India ink, the end of his days. At this point, Seba had done everything to prevent them from appearing. From hermetically closing each of his windows and buying biometric combination locks, to setting up a twenty-four-hour-a-day surveillance system to record his bedroom, his bedside table and his apartment, he felt he couldn't have done more.

Despite changing the camera position almost daily for the first two weeks, Sebastián could never explain why the footage did not capture the exact moment the notes appeared. In fact, the matter was even more mysterious, as there was no trace in the recordings of how the paper emerged. Apparently, the message of death that the notes carried was only visible to Seba. In any case, he was certain that he was not crazy and even suspected that there was something supernatural about the whole affair, especially when the origins of the letters were unprecedented. The camera managed to capture them for the first time as soon as Seba reached to grab them, even though he knew they were there long before he looked for them. To him, it was obvious that there was not even the possibility that they were placed by himself because, by the time they appeared, the physical distance between him and the nightstand was substantial. From the point of view of the security footage, the person placing the sheets of paper was either invisible, or so fast that the thirty-two frames per second that were continuously filmed were unable to catch them.

Regardless of the frequency with which Sebastián found the notes, he never considered notifying the police, for fear of being thought insane. The truth was that even he, as rational and smart individual, found the existence of an invisible ghost writer almost unbelievable. As a result, he began to feel the urge to escape from that arcane apartment in Old San Juan. For several weeks, he had been convincing himself of the possibility of moving to the old country lake house his parents had on the outskirts of San Juan, near Naranjito, between the towns of Corozal and Bayamón. In fact, he had thought so much about the matter that he had even told Violeta about his plans. Of course, he had never revealed to her the real reason for his urgency. This was because he wanted to preserve his image of lucidity in her eyes at all costs. In his gut, he knew that no matter how far he ran, the notes would still appear as timely as ever. Certainly, the world is not big enough to run from the misery of oneself. He'd become well aware of that, as on several occasions when he slept over on Violeta's couch, he would find the note upon awakening, on his right, waiting for him as always. As a consequence, moving to the lake house in the country was not a solution, but a futile attempt to escape from a future that every day seemed closer to fulfillment.

As they sat close together watching the *New York Ballet*, Sebastián continued to think about all the moves he had to make to move into the lake house. Although the place was available and ready, he estimated that it would take him at least a week and a half to make all the arrangements. This was because he needed to notify all his banks, the post office and his creditors about the change of address. He had to prepare his belongings for the move, sell a few leftover things and pack all his medical books, shoes, dress shirts, suits and other personal items. In addition, he had to contact a real estate agency to arrange for the sale of the apartment in Old San Juan, and he also had to notify (essentially asking permission from) his parents. Finally, he wanted to ask Doña Mama, who had been living there for several years to take care of the house, if she had any problem with him sharing her space. Honestly, these last two tasks regarding "asking permission" were the least of his worries, since his parents would surely agree and Mama was a sweetheart who never interfered with anything. By now long retired, she just watched her foreign-accented *telenovelas* and cleaned the whole place during the week. Proof of this was an occasion, a little over a year ago, when Seba stayed for several days in the house and only saw her when he got up, at which time she would prepare his breakfast and give him the daily blessing. During the rest of the day, her presence was not even felt.

As they left the theater, Sebastián was so quiet that Violeta felt lonely.

"Is something wrong with you?" asked Violeta.

"No, there's nothing wrong with me," there was silence for several seconds and he continued, "It's just that I've given more thought to the idea of moving to the country house and I've been making mental preparations for the move," Seba answered, a little afraid that she would uncover the real reasons for such a decision.

"I don't understand; why are you so determined to move?" asked Violeta as if she could read his mind.

"Nothing in particular," Dr. Pérez-Fuertes answered. "It's just that I need a change; I don't like the city anymore and I would prefer a new setting, just for a while."

"Honey, you're going to have to commute to San Juan every day for work—with a lot more traffic—and I'm going to continue to live and work here, so you'll still be surrounded by the same scenery except at night. Besides, it might even make it more complicated for us to see each other daily."

Sebastián knew that Violeta was absolutely right. In fact, the only reasonable explanation for wanting to move out of San Juan was the continued appearance of the perverse notes. For several seconds, which seemed like hours to both of them, he thought he could finally tell Violeta the truth. But, just before he opened his mouth, he decided to switch again to more excuses.

"My love, me moving out won't affect the fact that we see each other every day during the week. I have a studio apartment in the new office, where I can sleep over if I'm running late, or I could spend the night on your couch," said Seba without completely convincing Violeta.

"Yes, I know, but I'm still a little unhappy about the idea. Maybe it just took me by surprise, I don't know," said Violeta as she put her hand over her mouth and let out a long yawn.

"Anyway, it's not decided yet that I'm going to move, but you asked me about my silence so I shared my thoughts."

Once in front of Violeta's house, Sebastián accompanied her to the door, where they hugged, kissed and said goodbye. Although they had been dating for a little over two months, he and Violeta had talked and had decided not to be intimate until after they were married. That night was no exception.

On his way back, Sebastián reflected on his feelings. "I love her, I really do, in the purest way," he thought repeatedly. He didn't mind taking her as his virgin bride (as she had promised her father). She would be given away by her brother, Junior (whom he had not yet met due to some family squabbles between Violeta and him after her parents passed away, a topic she never wanted to discuss). Although they almost never spoke of Violeta's family, nor of her mother's illness, nor of the pain that followed her death, Sebastián knew that, until the last day of her life, Violeta would always be devoted to two things: to her promises and to the memory of Rocío Costas de Contreau. Moreover, he knew that she loved her so much that she would have remained single, for the rest of her life, if her mother had required it.

Hence, they loved each other in an innocent way, choosing to abstain from sex, basing their feelings simply on trust, mutual respect and friendship. They shared this rather pure relationship, which transported them to the most intimate confines of themselves. Unfortunately, this did not last forever; nothing does. That train of love would one day be diverted to the emptiest and darkest spaces of their souls.

∬Fourteenth

For Sebastián and Ian, Lake *La Plata* was always somewhat mystical. At first glance, it gave the impression of having the immensity of the Atlantic Ocean, the depth of the Caribbean Sea and the darkness of the Black Sea. Over its waters a world of mystery, almost of gloom, was projected. Under the surface though, it was a very quiet lake and, in its silence, small waves oscillated discreetly, hiding any secret buried in its confines. Although shy, that body of water was far from being asleep. If anyone dared to disturb its calm, it was ready to drag them into the abyss of its depths.

Right after they got married, the Pérez-Fuertes couple bought that property located west of San Juan, in a town between Corozal, Naranjito and Bayamón, in rural Puerto Rico. Now, almost six decades after his parents' marriage, Sebastián was standing right in front of the house, recalling many memories made in its hiding places. It had been three months since he had moved in. As he reminisced, he was transported back to the hundreds of times he and his brother ran like goats through the surrounding hills. Then he moved his memories to the Pérez-Laví wedding, between Ian and Dalymar, and the big reception party held by the lake; finally, he took a mental walk through his parents' golden anniversary celebrations and smiled with nostalgia.

"Nostalgia gives us the certainty that the past was worth it," he thought to himself.

As he wandered through his memories, Seba couldn't help but remember how much he had shared with his brother, Ian Samuel, during his childhood. He remembered their adventures around the lake, how neither its vastness, nor the abundant vegetation surrounding it had prevented their games or exploration. They both grew up there and, although they had not shared enough of it for years, that scenery framed the place where they had developed their strongest memories.

The house was immense and the lake formed a sort of peninsula around its roots. Above the entrance door, painted in sky blue, there was a plaque that read: *El Valle de los Pérez*. The mansion was built in two phases and remodeled on one occasion by Engr. Ian Samuel Pérez-Fuertes. The external structure was made of cement, with Spanish barrel type roof tiles, which gave it a different image from the Caribbean architecture of the mid-twentieth century. The exterior walls were painted light yellow and its roof edges retained the antique terracotta with which it was built. Inside it had an office and seven large bedrooms, which had never been occupied at the same time. In addition, there was a comfortable remodeled kitchen; a games room with a billiard table, a gigantic television and a bar; two nicely furnished living rooms; a piano next to a concert hall (full of dust); nine full bathrooms; a dining room, and numerous oil paintings by local artists. The Pérez-Fuertes home was built on the top of a small hill with the immense Lake *La Plata* below. From three sides of the house the view was of the lake. A small set of wooden steps served as a boardwalk. The boats were anchored at the end, next to a small shed where the fishing rods and aquatic equipment were kept.

Several months after moving in, Sebastián still hadn't managed to solve his problem of the unusual notes still appearing. Even though he had changed his zip code, they were still showing with the same regularity. The only difference was that they used to appear on his nightstand and now they appeared on his desk. By that date, Sebastián's calendar had already reached 147 consecutive days of letters appearing since he met Violeta. For him, this issue had begun to take on a tinge of desperation and he had become somewhat paranoid with each additional message he read. During his workdays, he was quite concerned about their possible veracity and there were times when he had to take an hour off to calm his nerves. When he was with Violeta, the very idea of losing her would ignite a feeling of terror that prevented him from enjoying every detail to the fullest. He felt as if those written words were the symptoms of a cancer, undiagnosed, growing inside his gut and unable to be treated or removed. He began to believe, with very little doubt, that he was running out of time. This is how the last few months had gone. Even worse, this was how the next six months of what would apparently be the end of his life could continue.

Once he returned from his tour of the past, Sebastián continued to silently observe every detail of the structure. He was still standing exactly in front of it, while his gaze wandered over the sharpness of its paint, the cleanliness of its surroundings and the freshness of the flamboyant orange trees. That smell of wild earth was unmistakable. It was this taste of nature, along with its green bushes, stone paths and the embrace of his memories that created a soothing atmosphere for Seba. "This is perfect," he thought to himself, "I wish one day I could share a home with Violeta in this house."

Once inside, Sebastián placed the food he had bought several hours ago in the kitchen counter. During that night, the number of encounters with Violeta would reach ninety-three dates in almost one hundred and forty-seven days. That night's prescription was calling for a romantic lakeside dinner under the moonlight. For this reason, he had meticulously chosen every detail of the meal. All that remained was to cook the dinner, set the table on the deck, place twenty or thirty oil lamps around the house and play soft music. Although he had been living in his parents' country house for some time now, he had not yet invited Violeta to see it. He had been waiting for the perfect moment and everything pointed to that night as the time to do it.

After he had finished organizing every detail of the romantic dinner, he quickly dressed, put a casual jacket over his linen button-down shirt and set off to pick up Violeta. When he arrived at her house, Sebastián remembered the day he met her. This was largely because Violeta had decided to wear the same black coat she had been wearing on that occasion. As a consequence, she had not come alone, as she was still carrying Carlos, the viral cold, right inside the right pocket of her coat.

"Honey, I know we had agreed that you were going to cook dinner, but I couldn't resist making a vanilla flan for dessert," said Violeta, biting her lower lip.

Seba had not made any preparations for dessert, so he had no problem with Violeta having done so.

"Are you kidding me? You know I love your flan and you, more than anyone, know me well enough to guess that I was going to forget dessert."

They smiled, kissed and continued towards the house. When they arrived, Violeta could not repress the enormous desire to tell Seba how much she liked it.

"It's so beautiful," said Violeta as she walked toward the sky-blue door of the house.

"I love it too but give it a little time and then you won't be so impressed, you get used to it," said Sebastián.

The truth was that there was no quick way to get used to it. For this reason, she could not hide the expression of astonishment in her eyes as she received a complete tour of the residence. After prowling through every nook and cranny of the mansion, they walked to the backyard and sat down to eat.

"I love you, sweetheart, thank you for dinner."

"You're welcome, darling, I love you too."

Throughout the night, Sebastián told Violeta of the memories he created in this house. He reminisced about all the summers he had spent there and the countless adventures he had with Ian. He described to her, in detail, the great time of drought when he was a boy that almost caused everything around him to disappear. He told her about so many things, but mostly just talked about the long afternoons he and his brother spent trying, unsuccessfully, to catch fish. She listened, attentively, to everything Seba told her and, from time to time, shared a memory related to the subject.

"Ah-choo!"

"Bless you."

"Thank you. I think I have a bit of a cold."

"Here, take my handkerchief."

Violeta wiped her nose, breathed in Seba's fragrance that was impregnated in the fabric and folded the handkerchief into four asymmetrical parts, before putting it in the right pocket of her coat. Actually, Miss Contreau did not have a cold; she had simply sneezed from the allergies created by the nature around her. But, to her misfortune, she had placed the handkerchief exactly where she was least supposed to if she wanted to keep her respiratory system free of Carlos. Throughout the night, Violeta was on the verge of reaching into her pocket for the reusable cotton tissue and blowing her nose; fortunately, she never got around to it. As a result, the virus came very close to dwelling inside someone again and thus being able to take over her feelings and actions. Unfortunately for him, his wish did not come true during that night. He was never able to be hosted by Violeta's body.

The dinner was exquisite, at least that was Violeta's opinion. The red wine was fresh and pure, the steak was tender and juicy, but the food was not the most delightful part of the evening. What really made up the moment was her smile and Seba's loving gaze, the fragrance of the countryside and the glow of the moon over the lake, whose light spread over their lips as they caressed each other.

"My love, I have one last surprise for tonight," said Sebastián in the middle of the evening.

"A surprise?"

"Yes, my love, and it depends on you to make it happen. Can you help me?"

"Sure," said Violeta as she smiled excitedly.

"Can you please reach under the chair and detach the envelope that is stuck there."

"Of course," she replied.

When she peeled it off, she had before her eyes a pink envelope that contained a small, square, white card.

"What are you waiting for, my love? Open it. Please, I know you are very good at guessing my intentions, so I'm going to need all your help here," said Seba.

Violeta found a small card that read,

"Violeta, would you do me the honor of m a_ r yi_ _ _e?"

Once she read it, Violeta burst into smiles and tears. When she looked at Seba, he was holding a red rose in his hands next to a black felt box with a very delicate ring inside.

"Violeta, will you do me the honor of marrying me?" asked Seba, kneeling down, while she read again the note in her hands.

"Yes, Sebastián, yes!" she answered.

Once these words were said, Violeta threw herself in his arms while repeating "Yes!" in his ear, with every tear and smile. Certainly, she had not imagined that during that night they would become engaged. Moreover, she never imagined she would love someone as much as she loved Seba.

Now engaged, they continued their dinner with a different feeling than at the beginning. Over Violeta's flan, they fantasized and planned details for their future. They talked about having two or three children. The first boy would be named Sebastián Luis in his honor. The first girl would be named Rocío in honor of Violeta's mother. They also talked about where they would live, whether in the city, in the suburbs or in the countryside. Although she and Seba both worked in San Juan, they agreed that they would not live in the capital for the first few years while raising their kids; they felt it was not the ideal place for this. In fact, they even considered raising them in the lake house, just as he and his brother had been raised.

In this way, they continued talking for several hours until the hands of the clock converged at 2:22 am. Once they realized this, they put the tableware in the sink and went to their bedrooms. Even that night, they did not sleep together.

In spite of the evening's merriment, when Violeta went to bed, she had a rather enigmatic dream, in which she found herself in a long, narrow hallway lined on all sides with red and yellow bedsheets. For no obvious reason, she was running at a fast pace toward a gigantic photo of her mother, which hung at the end of the hallway. The photo was so immense that it was about the size of a cargo truck. For some reason, she could not contain the urge to continue running towards it and, as she got closer, her breath became progressively heavier. Suddenly, deep within this nocturnal fantasy, she heard a great rumbling sound behind her that aroused her intrigue. When she turned around, she saw how the yellow and red blankets had begun to fall, blending together to form a range of colors that tended towards orange. Even though she could see everything crumbling before her, Violeta did not try to stop, but felt even more eager to reach her goal. However, no matter how hard she ran, the picture did not seem to get any nearer, but rather farther away as she tried to advance. Consequently, the photograph began to move at an impossibly fast speed, while her breathing became heavier, and the sheets in front of her path began to collapse right on top of her. Seeing this, Violeta came to a complete stop, but it was too late: she was trapped. Her body was surrounded by that sum of blankets that, slowly, were closing on her until they took away her strength to breathe, squeezing her neck little by little. With every second she became more and more convinced that she was going to die. Unexpectedly, just when she thought she would end up completely asphyxiated, she opened her eyes and found her body completely bathed in sweat, lying on the white covers of the guest room. Although she did not know the meaning of the dream, she felt that there was something more than a simple nightmare behind it, something beyond what she could explain.

Once she had recovered from that bad scare, Violeta went to the bathroom. When she came out, she found Sebastián in the kitchen. He had prepared a quick continental breakfast for her with fruits, coffee and toast. Ms. Contreau ate in total silence until she could no longer bear the weight of her anguish.

"My love, I had a nightmare," said Violeta.

"What did you dream about?" asked Seba.

"I don't know, it was pretty weird. As far as I can remember, I was running down a very long hallway full of yellow and red colored cloths or sheets. At the end of the corridor was like a huge picture of my mother, God rest her soul, and just as I was about to approach her, she sped away from me, as all the blankets wrapped around my neck and almost suffocated me. It was terrifying. I woke up out of breath, sweaty and with a very dry mouth."

"I understand, honey, but don't worry. It was probably a mechanism of your body to save your life. Let me explain, it could have been the case that your breathing was blocked by the sheet you were wrapped in or even by your own tongue or pharynx, if you were lying on your back and snoring. This obstruction of air could have caused your body, through your central nervous system, to create a dream or nightmare that was able to bring you out of that state and, as a consequence, save your life by waking you up and trying to allow the continuous passage of oxygen to your brain."

Because Dr. Pérez-Fuertes' answer sounded quite reasonable, she was more relaxed about the meaning of the dream. In fact, she was so satisfied with the explanation that she completely forgot about the fright produced by her nightmare.

Unfortunately, during that morning, Violeta contributed to the end of Carlos' days of leisure. For, just before leaving, she noticed that she still had Seba's handkerchief tucked away in her right coat pocket.

"Sebastián, I put your hanky on the dining room table, remember to wash it," said Violeta.

"Yes, no problem, I'll put it in the laundry when I get back."

Miraculously, the viral cold did not touch a single molecule of Violeta's body, passing from her pocket to the dining room table by means of the handkerchief. Unknowingly, Miss Contreau placed two things on the table that morning. The first was the piece of cloth folded in four that belonged to Sebastián and the second was a major piece of the final puzzle of their lives.

∬Fifteenth

A little more than three hours after Sebastián and Violeta left, Doña Mother and Don Samy arrived at the lake house. The idea for the visit came from the aged Dolores Fuertes, who had hopes to surprise her son in some compromising position while staying with his girlfriend. Unfortunately for her, she did not have the chance to find her son, and now future daughter-in-law, at the house. Regardless, they took the opportunity to relax and spend a few days enjoying the nice weather.

In their way, they had stopped by Ian's house to see how he was doing and to chat for a while. Their elder son was still the same as ever, with his home fairly immaculate inside and his building totally neglected on the outside. Unfortunately, he was having rat problems inside his apartment so he had had to call in pest control who had placed numerous consignments of rodent poison around the place. To his misfortune, a mother rat, "Doña Rata", as he used to call her, had masterfully delivered her twenty rodent babies somewhere in his apartment. As a result, he had an extra twenty-one unsolicited visitors residing in his place. Despite his battle with the trespassers, Ian Samuel was in perfect health.

Predictably, Doña Mother began to talk about how much she missed Daly and how much she knew he must be suffering because of her death. Ian Samuel, for his part, had no problem with this. Probably because he actually saw Dalymar on a daily basis. So, after two hours of visiting and prying into all his financial affairs, building plans and non-existent interpersonal relationships, the engineer's mother decided it was time to leave to visit Seba.

Objectively, upon arriving at the lake house, Doña Mother and Don Samy found everything in order. Without even a speck of dust on the floor, the house was clean. Of course, this was due to the fact that, to a great extent, Doña Mama was in charge of cleaning and had tidied once Seba and Violeta left. But there was something heterogeneous in that panorama, a detail that had the purpose of being there, waiting to be disturbed. Still, motionless, with an air of desperation to be touched, was the handkerchief placed by Violeta on the table. Once Doña Mother became aware of its presence, she fed on its existence to begin one of her ridiculous fights. Somehow, she had just decided that the house was a total mess and that everything around her was a pestilent dumpster.

"Look over there, you leave the house for a couple of months and this is how you find it, in total disarray. It is disgusting to arrive somewhere and find someone's dirty handkerchief on the dining room table. What's more, Doña Mama is going to have to give me a good explanation for this unpleasant gift, and she better not say that there is no problem, that this can be fixed very quickly, as she always does, or else I'll lose my mind. Because I swear on the soul of my father, the great Ramón Fuertes, that I'll throw her out of the house like a garbage bag. This... this is utterly disrespectful and I will not allow it. One, as a wealthy woman of high society, trusting in the service of others, having an image of a clean and neat lake house, well cared for, and when one arrives one finds a dumpster in total putrefaction. I tell you one thing, Samuel, a handkerchief on my dining table is as grotesque as a cockroach in my food...."

Doña Mother continued arguing alone for several minutes until Don Samy dared to interrupt her.

"Dolores, calm down, it's really not as disgusting as you say. Woman, if it makes you feel better, I'll pick it up myself and put it in the laundry room. Oh, and by the way, don't even think about yelling at Doña Mama because she is the sweetest person and the rest of the house is immaculate. Besides, she is not your slave or one of the servants, she is family, period."

"This is not what I needed, to have my authority over this house stripped away from me," Doña Mother pretended to cry and hurried to her room.

Don Samy then looked to his left and winked at Hidoki. Then he walked to the table and grabbed the hankie, which he placed in the left pocket of his shirt. Once in his possession, Carlos did everything in his power to be able to slip out and fall right where he wanted to, inside Sgt. Pérez's respiratory system.

In a matter of forty-eight hours, the virus moved from his hands to his nose, then traveled through his throat and settled nicely in his lungs. Once it entered his chest, it began its work of replication so that it could spread and take over everything within. Despite the fact that he had been out of action for more than two dozen years, Carlos quickly adapted to his new host. Unfortunately for the poor old man, well over eight decades old, his immune system was not prepared for such an invasion. During the first few days he began to feel a rather high fever, untamed by over-the-counter medications, which kept him in bed under the instructions of his son, Dr. Pérez-Fuertes.

"Water, give me water, I'm suffocating," cried Samuel, full of anger, "Don't you realize that I'm sick, that I'm not just lying in bed relaxing? Blessed be God and damn the hour when I decided to have two children as useless as the ones I've had, not to mention a wife who does nothing but go shopping and color her hair. A lifetime of working in the military to give them everything, a good education, an easy life, and look at me here, being treated like dirt and not even being listened to."

It was obvious that something had taken hold of Sgt. Samuel L. Pérez's lips. He was usually a very tender, humble, kind old man, quite calm and affectionate in his home. He never uttered a foul word, let alone insulted any member of the family. But now he could only be heard yelling at people and making them feel bad about their existence. He would bring out every flaw they wanted to hide and magnify them, times infinity, in order to humiliate them. Apparently, the secondary symptoms produced by Carlos' invasion were wreaking havoc not only on his host, but also on his loved ones. This was due to the neuronal predilection of this cunning bug, which usually nested not only in the lungs, but also in the left frontal lobe of the brain of its victims, causing all sorts of personality changes. Throughout his illness, Carlos took it upon himself to unleash the fury of his lack of hosts for more than two decades, intensified by his unwarranted captive laziness, and named Don Samy as the incriminating author of his woes.

Although he was nursed with great care by his younger son, Don Samuel failed to respond to any treatment. As the days went by, the diagnosis of a simple cold turned into pneumonia with bronchitis and, despite continuous hydration, nebulizers, chest x-rays, visits to the pulmonologist and preventive antibiotics, along with steroids, it turned into a wicked, superimposed, bacterial pneumonia. Don Samy never got to tell Seba, but he feared that his body was resisting the treatment plans due to the ravages of his previous pneumococcal infection, acquired on the Asian battlefields.

"Achoo-choo-choo-choo!" sneezed Samuel, haunted by a pain that started in his throat, passed through his esophagus and spread to his lungs. "Damn it, I hope the devil takes you all, go ahead and make me feel good, damn it! Sebastián, didn't you learn anything in medical school, or did they only teach you to give cough syrup? You are good for nothing; you are a useless son!"

In spite of all the expletives, Sebastián never stopped attending to him or caring for him with devotion. This was because part of his training as a physician included dealing, mentally, with the insults flung by others because of their pain. Indeed, a medical education teaches you to swallow hard, be empathetic and always turn the other cheek. Despite his screams and the seriousness of his infection, miraculously, no one, with the exception of his father, contracted the virus.

By this time, almost nine months of notes written in India ink had passed. Certainly, the situation had insidiously taken over Sebastián's mood. Despite the fact that they were already engaged to be married in the upcoming year, Seba rarely spoke about it. This was because, once someone started talking about the future, his gorge would rise and he would start to act differently, as he felt as if his wedding day would never come, putting complete truth in the weight of the message in the mysterious notes. Sometimes he would quickly calm down and sometimes he would simply mumble foul words that were more like barking than grumbling. In fact, it was because of this that the first arguments broke out between the couple. But not one of them affected their feelings for each other. Both continued to love one another until the last breath of their existence.

Sebastián was a gastroenterologist, not a pulmonologist or intensivist, but he did everything possible to save his father's life. As soon as he realized that his dad was not responding to medications, he decided to hospitalize him to prevent him from decompensating (contrary to what his colleagues suggested). Once he was admitted to the hospital, he sent him for at least a hundred additional test and cultures, ordered CT scans and added serological studies. He then demanded an infectious diseases team, along with pulmonologists from the University of Puerto Rico School of Medicine and even presented his case to the medical grand rounds, while he made all the arrangements to transfer his father to the Veterans Affairs Hospital in San Juan. Once stabilized and requiring lower levels of oxygen, he left him there, in expert and qualified hands. It took several days but it was only then that they discovered what was going on, after a direct examination of his lungs under video bronchoscopy. Sgt. Samuel L. Pérez not only had a viral pneumonia, complicated by a superimposed bacterial one, but he also had a metastatic cancer that had spread from his lungs across his body. In other words, the doctors found that he had lung cancer that initially looked like a pneumonia. Because of this, antibiotics had not completely cured him and would never do so. By the time the oncologists managed to get nuclear and tomographic images of his whole body, they realized that unfortunately it had spread to all his vital organs: from his lungs to his brain, and even his liver was involved. For this reason, Don Samy had no more than a couple of weeks or months to live, at the most, if he responded to a strong chemotherapy regimen.

Once they received the final diagnosis, Don Samy's decision, under the influence of Carlos, was to refuse all chemotherapy treatments and accept terminal, hospice care. He also signed a document refusing to be resuscitated or placed on a ventilator if he ever needed it. In reality, he had far, far less than six months to live. Undoubtedly, Sebastián had no choice but to initially accept his decision; certainly, there was no other dignified way, in his mind, to let him die. Subsequently, his dad asked to be transferred to the lake house, under the care of his son and a graduate nurse. This was fulfilled to the letter, as Sgt. Pérez had every right to choose his own destiny.

Upon learning of his father's diagnosis, Sebastián held a meeting in the hospital waiting room with his brother and mother.

"Doña Mother, Ian, the old man is sicker than we thought," said Sebastián with a lump in his throat and his eyes red with tears.

As he continued talking, he explained to both of them, in simple terms, the condition that Don Samy had. In spite of how delicately he told them, Doña Mother was stunned and had no reaction whatsoever, other than to remain with her eyes wide open; then she froze and collapsed on the couch in the waiting room.

"Seba, what's wrong with her?" asked Ian as he tapped her on the shoulder trying to get her to react.

"I don't know, she must have gone into a state of anxiety or panic," Seba answered as he took her pulse and listened to her breathing. His hands found her cold and covered in sweat.

"Well, do something, I don't want to be motherless too!" Ian shouted.

With that said, Seba began to run in search of more doctors to help him. When he returned, he came back with two other physicians and three nurses who took her vitals, put her in a wheelchair and transferred her to the emergency room, where they did CT scans of her head, EKGs, blood tests and all came back, satisfyingly, just fine. They believed that she was in a state of absolute panic, just as Sebastián had initially suspected. As a result, they decided to sedate her and admit her to the hospital under observation. Once they finished filling out the hospital admission paperwork, they said goodbye to her, their father (who was still a patient in another room while waiting for his own arrangements) and went home.

In less than two days, Ian and Sebastián made all the preparations to take Sgt. Pérez to the lake. They hired a registered nurse and fully fitted out one of the rooms for him. They also stocked up on all the medical equipment Seba thought necessary and filled the house with family photos to set the mood.

Despite the many preparations they made for their father's arrival, they never conceived of having to make arrangements for Doña Mother's arrival as well. When they went to visit her the next day, they found her yelling at the doctors and demanding that they call her son because "he was a real doctor" and "not an inept quack doctor like them." The truth was that she had been quite upset by the news of her husband's imminent departure. The very idea of losing the only person who had stayed by her side day and night for the past six decades and a fraction was shocking enough to throw anyone's world off balance. No matter how long it had been from the moment they swore eternal love to each other, they both still loved the memory of the first day, the throbbing of the first kiss on the tree swing, the births of their two children and the image of youth they perceived as they looked into each other's faces. Regardless of the eighty-odd years of old age they carried in their eyes, they still loved each other, deeply.

Thankfully, Sebastián was present when Doña Mother's madness reached its critical point. It was only then that the doctors were able to convince her to take the sedatives.

"I'm not going to take a single pill that you don't put in my mouth," shouted Doña Mother to Seba, totally unrestrained.

"I know, I know, that's why I'm here, to take care of you myself," Sebastián replied as he placed the medicine in her mouth.

From that moment on, Doña Mother's sanity continued to decline. Three days after the first incident at the hospital, the psychiatrists released her to return home. Once they were able

to calm her down, they made a few arrangements so that, like
Don Samy, she would be more comfortable under Seba's care.
In spite of how much she insulted and mistreated Doña Mama
throughout her life, it was the latter who took care of her boss
until the end of her lucid days.

∫∫Sixteenth

On the night of the three hundred and thirty-second consecutive letter, Dr. Sebastián L. Pérez-Fuertes had the penultimate omen of the end of his life. The dream was so vivid that he could perceive the bloody cough that slipped through his teeth. He was in a different place, covered with giant trees, surrounded by very dark, green mountains. As he looked ahead his eyes registered an Asian man with a knife stuck in the center of his chest. As soon as he became aware of his presence, he tried to scream and run away, but remained motionless and mute. When he finally mastered his senses, his mouth was only able to emit a string of sounds that sounded more like moans than danger alerts. On the Asian's head was a conical straw hat. His wound was lethal, he knew because the way the knife went in, surely, it had to have shattered the right atrium of his heart and the aorta. But, even knowing that the man was dead, he could not resist the urge to talk to him. Under the light of that unknown night sky, he told him his surname and first name, told him about his family, his ranks within the U.S. Army and how much he hated the Korean War. For some reason, he answered questions that didn't exist, laughed at jokes that were never made. He didn't really know exactly where they were, but no matter the name of that unknown jungle, it wasn't part of any of the towns in Puerto Rico he had ever visited, that much he knew. Instinctively, he looked at his body and realized that, once again, it was not him, but the same dispirited man he had impersonated in his dreams during that military ball nightmare, almost eleven months ago. Suddenly, his chest cavity began to tighten and his breathing became sharper, while his lungs felt the stabbing entry of pain shooting through his alveoli and out through his back. He coughed so hard and often that he was hunched over his knees, his eyes closed and his body became thirsty for oxygen. Seven, eight, nine seconds went by and, at the tenth count, he felt his chest relax and breathe that air that turned his anguish into glory. As he recovered from the coughing fit, he looked around and noticed that he was no longer in that unknown jungle but was lying on a bed in a rather dark room. Although it took him a couple of seconds to get his bearings, he was able to decipher that he was in one of the rooms of the lake house. He moved his head and noticed the tubes over his face, connecting him to an oxygen tank. He looked down at his arms and felt the bruises on his aged hands. When he looked to his right, he found the presence of the same Asian man he had been talking to, who still had the knife stuck in the center of his chest. As soon as he looked into his eyes, he noticed that his companion began to walk towards the door of the room. Almost in sync, he ripped off the artificial oxygen, along with the sheets, and followed the stabbed man out of the bedroom. He felt as if chasing him was his destiny. Even though the moon was pointing towards the late hours of the evening, he continued walking through the house, crossed over the grass dampened by the night dew and descended the steps of the boardwalk that led down to the Lake *La Plata*. Once he reached the end of the path, he watched as his companion plummeted into the water. Several moments later, he followed.

As he woke up, Sebastián let out a deafening scream. Terrified, he began to run wildly towards the outskirts of the house and in the direction of the lake. Once he got there, he was struck dumb when he recognized the presence of two distinct footprints, produced by the grass and its dew, leading to the edge of the walkway. Sebastián began to run again while his eyes combed the water to see if he could find his father at any point; he saw nothing. When he reached the end of the tracks, he stopped and desperately searched for some clue as to where to jump. Sebastián did not notice, due to the darkness of the night, but the hue of the water had changed. It was no longer greenish-brown, but had turned a dark wine color that gave it the appearance of stagnant blood in a deadly basin.

"Dr. Pérez, Dr. Pérez, come quick, he's dying!" shouted the nurse from the courtyard of the house.

Sebastián then began to run towards Don Samy's room. "Surely," thought Seba as he ran, "the old man jumped into the lake and managed to swim to shore. Then, probably, the nurse called me when she saw him wet and gasping with bronchospasms." Unknown to Dr. Pérez was that his father's body was not suffering from the complications of diving into the water in the middle of the night, but was going through the final moments of a death catalyzed by his lung cancer.

To his surprise, when he entered Don Samy's bedroom, he found him completely dry, with his oxygen mask and tubes perfectly connected. Totally opposite to his initial hypothesis regarding the origin of the emergency.

"The old man is dying, call the ambulance!" Seba shouted when he saw his father in bed completely purple, ignoring that he wanted to die at home, without returning to the hospital, under the palliative terminal services of his son.

Because Samuel no longer had a pulse and the oxygen mask didn't do his lungs much good, Sebastián decided to pull the plug and take the rest of what was left of his life into his own hands. Although he was aware that his father did not want to be resuscitated or put on any mechanical ventilation machine, he refused to let him die. Almost instinctively, he began to run the advanced cardiovascular life support protocols he knew by heart. He opened his lips, moved his jaw down and began to provide mouth-to-mouth resuscitation.

"One thousand one, one thousand two, one thousand three, one thousand four, one thousand five," Seba shouted as he transferred his air into Don Samy's lungs and the nurse established intravenous access.

"Epinephrine, atropine, IV or subcutaneous," he yelled to the nurse. He also asked her to find him the resuscitation machine. But there was no resuscitation machine in his house, he knew that. In Seba's mind every minute that passed increased the medical certainty that his father would not live, that he would probably have brain damage if he did, and that there was little point in his efforts since he was essentially dead. Still, he refused to give up.

"Papi, react, react, old man, please," said Seba while he kept flexing his hands on the inert chest resting under his arms. "Breathe, you can't die today. Don't die, old man, not here, not now, not in my arms. Come back, please, come back!"

Thirty minutes after starting his resuscitation, when the paramedics arrived, they found Sebastián still trying to revive the cold, stiff and dead body, while repeating out loud:

"It's not true, you're not dead, I know you're still alive."

Upon seeing this, the emergency services team took charge of separating Seba from the body, checked Don Samy's non-existent vital signs, read the *Do Not Resuscitate / Do Not Intubate* papers provided by the nurse, and ended the code blue.

On the night of the three hundred and thirty-second consecutive letter written in black India ink, Don Samuel Luis Pérez passed away. Certainly, his son should never have tried to resuscitate him. That was not what he wanted, but Sebastián could not accept it.

Despite dying of respiratory failure, Don Samy did not feel any pain in his final moments. He only concentrated on feeling the white frost that spread between his fingers on the Korean soil and gave thanks, repeatedly, for not having died, physically, during that war.

Two more letters were delivered between his father's death and his funeral. At the last farewell were Ian (together with Dalymar, in her metaphysical state), Sebastián, Violeta, Doña Mother, Doña Mama, Natalia with her husband, several close friends of the Pérez-Fuertes family and some other comrades from the 65th Infantry who were still alive in body (*gold* listed). In addition to the guests there were four young officers, military men totally unknown to all present. After Father Rodrigo said his last words, prayers and phrases of support for the family, the casket of Dolores Fuertes' husband was lowered, while the shooting of the rifles from the four unknown soldiers could be heard. As soon as the last of the shots were heard, the sky unleashed its fury by bursting a string of lightning that would serve as a preamble to a tumultuous deluge. In the rain, the military men folded, in a triangular shape, an American flag that was not accompanied by their treasured Puerto Rican one with its white lone star. This other flag, with fifty different stars, was one that Sgt. Samuel Luis Pérez fought for all his life with respect, always considering it to be one of his greatest achievements and successes, just like the academic careers of his children and his six plus decades of marriage to his beloved Dolores. He always considered himself as proud to be an American as he was to have been born a pure *Boricua*. Knowing that this might happen, Don Samy had asked Sebastián to place a Puerto Rican flag inside his casket. Thus, the only semblance of homeland with which he would remain, during his eternity, would be that of being born in Borinquen.

Afterwards, the soldiers marched towards Doña Mother and presented her with that triangular souvenir, in honor of her husband's exemplary service during all his battles.

"Oh, Jesus Christ, tell me this isn't happening! Oh, God, I gave you a man and today you are exchanging him for a folded piece of cloth, please, return my husband to my arms!" cried Doña Mother under the rain, while the soldiers walked away.

During that afternoon, the last living part left inside the heart of Dolores Fuertes/Doña Mother, died. Never again was she heard to speak coherently or seen to smile. Much less was she seen returning to the Country Club or criticizing the whole world at the *El Popurrí* beauty salon. As time went by, her hair was showing the gray coat that for so many years had been disguised. Her skin, without make-up, revealed the deep wrinkles that made up her almost eight and a half decades of anger. Despite Doña Mama's excellent care and the prescribed drugs, Doña Mother showed no progress for almost three weeks. During these, she attempted suicide twice using giant pots of *acetaminophen*. After the second suicide attempt, Sebastián and Ian decided to listen to the psychiatrists and admit her to St. John's Psychiatric Hospital in San Juan, with the hopes that they could provide intensive help for her severe depression. The day she was admitted marked three hundred and fifty-five days of continuous letters. As Seba signed the last of the admission papers, he believed that someday he would see his mother come out sane again. The sobering truth would be that she would never leave that mental hospital, nor would any of her children ever see her again.

Throughout the days in which Doña Mother showed no progress, the water level in Lake *La Plata* grew considerably. No one noticed, but for almost three weeks straight since Don Samy's death it had rained daily at the same time that the triangular American flag had been given to his mother, as a patriotic exchange for her husband. Thus, the volume of the large basin of water (which now appeared to be dark orange/bloody red) began to rise to the point that it covered the top of the steps of the boardwalk. Little by little the *Pérez Valley* was giving way to its flood.

When they came home from the hospital, Seba arranged for Doña Mama to move into the apartment he had in Old San Juan, which he had not yet been able to sell despite his best efforts. The truth was that he wanted to be completely alone in the lake house. In addition to the notes, the recent death of his father and his mother's abrupt psychiatric collapse, had made him feel very fragile; therefore, he wanted to leave all his affairs in order. For this reason, after setting her up in his apartment in the city, he went with Doña Mama to his lawyer's office and changed the deeds to the apartment into the name of the woman who had so often acted as his mother in Doña Mother's absence. Apparently, the only thing left that he could not fix was the enigma that covered his life and that had taken over his temperament and thoughts. The following days that Sebastián lived were marked by bad moods, interrupted by a great sadness that, apparently, only further inflamed the state of nerves and the unstoppable progression of his actions to come.

♫ Seventeenth

The delivery of the prophetic notes was so diligent that Sebastián no longer even used the solar calendar to orient his days. That morning, his count was three hundred and fifty-seven letters since he had met Violeta. Seba had plenty of these premonitory messages, but even so, the note he would receive that morning would not be very pleasant. The night before he had gone to bed after 12:00 a.m., using the charms of the "ANTENNA" button to recreate a romantic evening he had spent with his fiancée. When he got up, he looked to his right and noticed that the usual note was missing from his desk. "Could the deliveries have stopped?" wondered Seba somewhat intrigued, "or could it be that I'm still asleep?"

Sebastián was not asleep, in fact, he was wide awake and there was no note on his desk. Unfortunately, his joy would not be long in disappearing for, looking over at his bed, he found a note written in India ink and lying face down on his other pillow. It read:

Your year of life is coming to an end

In itself, the note contradicted the pattern created over the past year. For one thing, it had appeared not to his right when he opened his eyes, but to his left, on the pillow he had not used. Second, it was the first time that any of the notes had spoken more explicitly about the end of the year, thus adding a little extra anxiety to its message. For this reason, Dr. Pérez-Fuertes could not help but be even more distressed by the persistence of the letters. He felt as if his life was marked by a cruel countdown in which the only certainty was the (apparently exact) day of his death.

That morning, after getting dressed, at 7:57 a.m., Sebastián decided to break his silence and tell his older brother everything that was happening to him. As he drove to Ian's apartment, his brain began to whirl around the hundreds of letters he'd received throughout the year; from the first note that took him to Paris, to this last one, which would prompt him to tell another human being for the first time. Next, he thought of Violeta and how much he loved her. But thinking about her involved more than touching her with his memories, since every moment relived in his thoughts increased that real fear of losing her someday, apparently very soon. If the letters were true, Seba had, by his inaccurate count, little more than a week to live. And, although a minute of life is still life, it was not great enough to satisfy his thirst for love with Ms. Contreau. For him, not even eternity would have been enough to fulfill such a purpose.

Thus, Sebastián Luis Pérez's mind was wandering between the final tally of his life, the hundreds of letters received, his fiancée and the agony of his possible forced separation. As his thoughts floated, his chest began to flood with a mixture of rage, dread and fear, which he was unable to distill. By the time he reached the front of Ian's apartment, his reason was totally deranged. His nerves had been saturated by more neurotransmitters than he needed and his thoughts had been contaminated by a progressive and terrifying psychosis.

The feeling of anger that Sebastián harbored was so great that he was alienated from everything that made up the structure of the *Les Pérez Apartments* complex. In fact, it was still as delipidated as ever. Once he parked his car, he walked toward his brother's apartment without noticing the jungle of weeds that covered the entrance. To him, none of this existed. Perhaps that's why he didn't flinch at the large battalions of insects trying to stop him in his tracks, nor did he pause at the huge *dengue fever* mosquito breeding grounds that flirted with being ponds. He was simply determined to talk to his brother regardless of whether the world stopped or kept on turning.

As he rang the doorbell, Sebastián had an odd feeling that something strange was going on. Unexpectedly, he heard several footsteps and instructions issued by Ian to someone he was not quite prepared to meet. While waiting to be let in, he had a premonition that there was something cryptic about their whispering and tardiness. He was completely paranoid, so much so that he began banging on the door in an attempt to catalyze his brother's arrival.

"Come on, open up, I'm in a hurry!" Seba shouted, as he tried to force his way into apartment #010b.

During the several minutes he had been waiting, Dr. Pérez-Fuertes recalled the mysterious beating Ian had received during the morning that Violeta had appeared in his life. But this was not what intrigued him most about the matter, rather how long he had had to wait during that day to enter the house and how intense the smell of perfume, mixed with blood, had been as he had treated him. His brain, in a frenzied fashion, began to elaborate a thesis that Ian was to blame for the notes. Without making any kind of sense of his assertions, Seba went so far as to create a pyramidal conspiracy theory. "Surely," he thought, "there are more people involved in all this."

In essence, his almost childish theory was based on the fact that there was a secret cult or sect conspiring to kill him, to intimidate him, or to drive him insane. It sounded completely crazy but, to him, this cult formed the base of the pyramid, while the thickness of the body was made up by the letters sent in black India ink and the apex was formed by Ian, who was in charge of finding ways to deliver them.

"Aha!" thought Seba again, "so that's why the notes kept popping up even when I moved to the lake house. Ian was always the rat spying on me." He thought about this, forgetting, in his accusatory madness, that the notes also appeared next to the couch when he slept over at Violeta's house; a place Ian didn't know.

For no compelling reason, his obsession with this theory reached astronomical levels, so high that by the time Ian appeared at the door to let him in, Seba's eyes were no longer dark brown, but the same bloody wine color that the lake had acquired since the night of his father's death.

"How are you?" asked Ian Samuel as he opened the door.

"I'll tell you how I am!" Seba answered, flooded with anger and by now feeling extremely agitated.

Once Sebastián's feet crossed the door frame, any reason remaining faded away.

"Where are they? Tell me! Where are they?" he shouted as he sniffed around every corner of the apartment, looking for a clue or an accomplice hidden by his brother.

But the younger of Don Samy's sons was not completely wrong in his conspiracy theories, for Ian was not entirely alone that day. Standing to his right was Dalymar, as radiant as ever. On the bedside table in Ian's room was Ernie, whose image could be seen through the half-open door to the living room. In addition to Ernie and Daly, that evening Don Eugenio and Don Juan were sitting in their usual seats in Ian's house. For Sebastián, the presence of all of them was nil. But he continued to scrutinize every inch of his brother's apartment for clues and culprits.

He looked under his bed, in the bathroom, over the sink; he found nothing. He snooped in the coffee jar, inside the refrigerator, in the cupboard; nothing. Inopportunely, just when his yelling began to die down, he found something that fueled his anger and multiplied his suspicions.

On Ian's drawing table were three bottles of India ink, which he always used to hand-sign his final work. The instant Seba noticed the bottles, his sweat-drenched face disfigured into the image of an unhinged bull, ready to charge at the world at the slightest provocation. According to him, he had found the corpus delicti.

"So, you think my last year of life is running out, huh? You piece of shit! Where are they? Tell me, damn it! Where are they?" asked the angry, sweating bull with wine-colored eyes.

"Where are who? What do you mean? Your last year of life is running out, are you sick, what's wrong with you?"

"Ian, don't act foolish, these bottles prove that you are involved in all this," Seba shouted, pointing at them.

"What are you talking about? That's nothing more than the ink I use to sign my finalized engineering plans."

"That's not it, stop lying! Just confess you used that ink to write the notes you have been delivering on behalf of your diabolical sect."

"What are you talking about? Diabolical sect? What notes? What on earth are you talking about, man?" asked Ian, totally disoriented.

Apparently, the phrase "diabolical sect" had an exponential effect on Seba's anger, because as soon as he repeated it, he hunched completely over, touching his abdomen with his knees, and from his mouth began to come out a kind of loud, constant roar. In addition, his lips began to drip a thick fluid composed of saliva, phlegm and snot, while both his fists closed hermetically.

After a couple of minutes in this pose, Sebastián stood up and began to smash everything in his path by tossing it wherever. He started with his brother's laptop, which landed on the living room TV. Then he moved to the kitchen, where he emptied the shelves without leaving a single piece of crockery intact. But the height of his fury was reached when he grabbed his brother's blueprints and tore them into pieces, then stuffed them into his mouth and chewed them in desperation. Finally, he grabbed the three bottles of India ink and used them as projectiles.

Throughout the entire outburst of madness, Ian had remained petrified, standing in the same position he had been in when his apparently possessed brother entered his apartment. None of Ian's visitors had moved either, they were all witnessing the explosion of feelings Sebastián was experiencing.

The first of the India ink bottles landed on a small portrait of Albert Einstein that Ian had hanging on one of the walls of his living room. The second throw hit Ian's left hand which, fortunately for him, got in the way of the impending collision with his face. Unfortunately, the last bottle was the most lethal of all, though, and became the fire that would destroy Ian's imaginary fortress of happiness. Without even looking where he was throwing it, Sebastián released the last projectile and watched, with his eyes full of vengeance, its trajectory.

In less than a couple of seconds Ernie's figure had fallen broken into a thousand pieces on the floor of apartment #010b.

Almost instantly, Ian collapsed onto the floor. His countenance took on an air of grief and his eyes became the channels of a continuous, unceasing sea of tears.

"No!" cried Ian from the bottom of his heart, "What have you done, Seba?" were the last words Ian would say in his lifetime.

Suddenly, Don Eugenio and Don Juan began to fade from their seats as they waved goodbye with their aged hands. Then Ian looked at Daly and saw how she blew him a kiss from a distance and told him, in a mute voice, that she would always love him. At that moment, Dalymar Laví's body vanished forever into the void.

Seeing her leave without him, Ian got up from the floor, walked to his room and sat on his bed, completely silent.

"Speak, don't be so dramatic!" shouted Sebastián as he sat up. "I warn you, Ian, I'm not physically hurting you because you're my brother, but if I find even one more of those letters, I swear I'll beat you up worse than the beating you got for the married woman cheating business."

Dr. Pérez-Fuertes then left the apartment and started his vehicle. After he left, Ian sat for several hours on his bed, reflecting on all that had happened, until he finally decided to end his solitude.

∫∫Eighteenth

"Hail Mary most pure."

"Conceived without sin."

"Father, forgive me for I have sinned."

Violeta had just sat down in the confessional at St. John's Cathedral. She had arrived in the middle of the morning, straight from the library, wrapped in a blanket of eternal guilt.

"Tell me daughter, how have you sinned?"

"I finally found my mother's murderer," Violeta replied, as she raised her head to reveal a face full of silent tears.

"Your mother's murderer? How is that possible? She wasn't murdered!"

Technically, Father Rodrigo was absolutely right. Violeta's mother had died eleven months and some weeks ago, due to cardiac arrest, caused by lack of oxygen and internal bleeding, as a complication of a colonoscopy. At least, that was what her death certificate stated. The Contreau-Costas family did not fully accept this explanation. For them, her death could have been postponed or, at least, diligently attended to, without causing her to suffer.

"He killed her, Father, he killed her. And the worst thing is that he probably doesn't even know it. The saddest thing is that she probably meant nothing to him...," she said with her head bowed.

"Violeta, calm down and tell me, who do you think killed your mother. Do you want me to call the police?" he asked almost without waiting for her to finish.

To understand this interaction between Father Rodrigo and Violeta, one had to pause and turn back the clock to earlier that morning. Hours earlier, Ms. Contreau woke up in high spirits. Then she dressed, put on perfume and took the bus to the San Juan Municipal Library where she worked. Her punch card read 8:01 a.m. At that time, she walked to her desk to begin her daily tasks. Just over an hour after arriving, the phone on her desk rang once... twice... three times... until, at 9:11 a.m., she answered the call.

"Hi, is this Violeta Contreau?" asked her brother on the other end of the phone.

"Junior? How are you? What a miracle that you call me without asking for my forgiveness!"

"I'm fine, but I'm calling to give you some good news. Yes, I apologize for the stupid fights, I'm so sorry. Now, let's move on from them in peace. Guess what, sis?"

"What do I have to guess?"

"Well, what happened with the medical malpractice claim that you never wanted to know about and from which you are now going to benefit very handsomely, thanks to your quasi-lawyer brother."

Junior had contacted Violeta just after receiving a call that morning from his boss at the law firm where he worked as a paralegal. It turned out that the malpractice insurance company had reached a monetary settlement with the Contreau-Costas family, all in an effort to avoid going to trial. The settlement made it very clear that, although the death of Rocío Costas de Contreau had not been intentionally caused, the company did admit the moral obligation to pay a monetary sum for the damages that the occurrence of her death may have induced in them.

It had been almost a year since she had spoken to Junior, after a rather virulent argument they had following their mother's death. During that dispute, her brother yelled at her demanding his inheritance money, specifically, trying to convince her to sell their late mother's house, which had been left by Doña Rocío to Violeta. She, of course, refused to sell it. Since then, they had not talked at all. Now, on the other end of the line was her brother, full of greed, telling her the details of the deal. In short, as part of the settlement, the insurance company prohibited them from (1) suing anyone again for the incident and (2) making any public comments that included the name of Dr. Sebastián L. Pérez-Fuertes, his Gastroenterology Clinic or the insurer in any public statement.

As soon as her brother said that name, Violeta felt as if the whole weight of the universe had fallen on her chest.

"Repeat the name again, Junior. Just repeat the name again," Violeta shouted from the other end of the phone.

"Calm down, Violeta, the name of the doctor we are suing is Dr. Sebastián Luis Pérez-Fuertes. We sued him under the name of his Gastroenterology Clinic, but that is the doctor responsible. Our arguments were that she died because, by not being present in his office on the day of her follow-up visit for Mami's colonoscopy, after his staff checked her in, he made her wait too long and did not even show up at his office at all. Don't you remember? Anyway, it doesn't matter, because it seems that they finally realized that mom would be alive if that "shitty doctor" had attended her when it was her turn, without leaving her alone for so many hours in his waiting room, which led to her exsanguinating and dying.

The sound of her fiancé's name was able to pierce Violeta's ears so violently that it reached her throat, where she felt as if a great blow of guilt had fallen, passing through her esophagus and landing in her stomach. Actually, there was a possibility that she might never have known that Sebastián was the gastroenterologist who treated her mother. But, if true, it was as if fate had set a trap for them, since all the pieces were in place for it to happen. First of all, Violeta didn't even remember that her brother had hired a lawyer, essentially because he had hired his boss at the law firm where he worked. Worse, she never accompanied her mother to doctor's visits, because Junior was the one who was in charge of taking her to her daytime appointments, and that was a routine follow-up one after her colonoscopy. She believed that her mother had died waiting for her primary care physician, Dr. Santiago, nor did it occur to her that she had died at the Gastroenterology Office located on Buendía Street at the corner of San Damián. Even if she had known the address, that same week they had opened the new office, so there really was no way she could have known. In addition, Violeta never had the opportunity to meet the doctor who performed the colonoscopy on her mother. This was because, at the time this all happened, Dr. Pérez-Fuertes was so undedicated to his profession that he never visited his patients after hours, let alone at the hospital. Finally, she refused to have anything to do with the lawsuit her brother orchestrated because, to her, it was vindictive and unchristian; in fact, she thought he had never pursued it. Sadly, even if she had been involved in the malpractice suit, it would have been quite difficult for her to know that it was her fiancé's, since there were at least fifteen gastroenterologists named Dr. Pérez in San Juan, Puerto Rico, causing more confusion in the whole matter.

Once her brain digested her reality, Miss Contreau was struck dumb and felt her whole being freeze from the outside to the inside of her chest, coming to a shuddering halt in her heart and letting her feel the fullness of the palpitations that set its rhythm. Heartbeat after heartbeat, she relived the memories of love shared with her mother, including her first communion, her nights as a child during the Christmas holidays and the thousands of daily memories with her. She also recalled the sad moments, the nights spent in the hospital with her and her father after he was diagnosed with advanced pancreatic cancer. She remembered so many things, including that her mother was her best friend. Images of Doña Rocío began to intertwine with memories with Sebastián. Then she discovered the cruelty of her predicament, as she realized that, if what her brother just said was true, she loved every detail of the man who murdered her mother. She loved watching him sleep and kissing his lips. She was obsessed with hearing him laugh and whispering "I love you"; she loved hugging him tightly and keeping him by her side, since he made everything around her world much happier. She loved him; oh, how much she loved him! And this was something incapable of being erased, even if she knew it would be impossible for her to forgive him. If this was all true, how sad and dark her future would be! For surely there is no greater punishment than to love someone you also hate. Her heart was left in ruins, shattered.

After she'd finished talking with her brother, Violeta could not find a way to erase the guilt from her skin. She could not find an algorithm capable of scrubbing the blood from her hands and fingers; she could not silence the screams that resounded inside her conscience. She loved the man who snatched her mother from the present and buried her in the past; she hated the very thought of the person who taught her how to love again and gave a new meaning to her life.

A few minutes after Junior's call, Violeta decided that she could not live with her grief and decided to go to St. John's Cathedral to confess and talk to Father Rodrigo.

So, after explaining what had happened that morning, we find ourselves back in the confessional.

"My mother's murderer is called," Violeta paused and burst into tears. As hard as she tried, it took her several seconds to recover.

"Take your time, daughter. I know it must be extremely painful for you."

"You said it but you can't know, Father," she answered between murmurs and gasps.

Quietly, she remained in tears until she suddenly paused and said,

"Sebastián, my fiancé, killed my mother, unintentionally, but still he was responsible for her death."

"God forbid, daughter! Why are you saying this? I myself married Samuel and Dolores, then I baptized the children and neither of them would be able to do such a thing. Well, maybe perhaps Dolores could do it..., but that's not the point. For sure Sebastián would never do it, he is a doctor! Besides, you love each other, why would you think such a thing?"

"Sebastián killed her, Sebastián killed her..., Junior told me today on the phone," Violeta continued repeating as her words broke and came together again.

"Junior? How does he know that? Are you sure?"

"I don't know if it's one hundred percent true, but Junior doesn't even know him yet. We haven't spoken in almost a year because of the arguments over the house and inheritance details," she answered with her eyes lost in space.

There was a pause, many tears, and then she began to speak again.

"As I told you, Father, my brother called me earlier this morning, after having spoken with the lawyer from his law firm, whom he hired on his own behalf. He was the one who told me that Dr. Sebastián L. Pérez-Fuertes, a gastroenterologist in San Juan, had indirectly killed her," said Violeta, as she let out another cry.

"Calm down, daughter, surely it was a misunderstanding. You'll see that soon everything will be all right."

"Unfortunately, there is nothing to fix, Father. Everything is very clear," Violeta got up and left without saying goodbye to her confessor.

ʃʃNineteenth

That morning on which his inexact calendar marked the three hundred and fifty-seven consecutive letters, an immense traffic accident had occurred that delayed Sebastián from returning back to his office from Ian's house. Once the paramedics, the victims, the five ambulances, the twelve police cars, the vehicles of people wanting to see what happened, cleared out of the avenue, the clock on the semi-automatic red car that Seba was driving showed 10:02 a.m.

Sebastián entered his office in a totally frayed mood. Not only had he argued fiercely with his brother, but he had to wait for almost an hour in traffic thanks to the car crash. When he walked in, he looked at Natalia and realized that something unusual had happened.

"What's the matter?" asked Seba, still irritated.

"We'd better talk calmly in your office," replied Nata as she followed him to his desk.

"Did something happen to your husband?"

"No, Sebastián, this has nothing to do with me or my husband."

As Natalia said these words, Violeta was exiting through the doors of the cathedral and was on her way to the corner grocery store to buy a box of matches and every single one of the thirty-four candles with saints painted on their sides, that were left for sale. On the other side of town, Nata continued her conversation with Seba.

"The malpractice insurers called today, saying that your policy was voided and that they submitted your file to the Puerto Rico College of Physicians to revoke your license."

"But why? I haven't been sued in a long time. What's more, you well know that I have never in my life loved what I do so much. I have been spotless for almost a year now."

"Sebastián, I know that well, and I'm glad of it; actually, I'm quite proud of you. But the insurance company had to pay a substantial amount of money in order to close the last case of malpractice reported to you."

"When was this? Was there a new lawsuit? You know very well that the last time I was accused of malpractice was more than a year ago."

"No, it was exactly three hundred and sixty-four days ago," corrected Natalia.

"No, no, it was much longer ago. What's more, the gentleman's name was... was... I forget the name. What matters is that it's been over a year since it happened. I've even paid the policy twice during that time."

"Yes, you are partly right. It was a "gentleman" named Rocío Costas de Contreau," Natalia answered sarcastically as she read the fax that had been sent to her from the insurance company.

As soon as he heard Violeta's mother's name, Sebastián felt the impact of guilt in his muscles. Natalia continued speaking, but her words were no longer audible. Suddenly, a mixture of fury, fear and dread was diluted and transformed into immense anguish, provoked by the news he had just received. Likewise, his eyes turned jet brown again and his face lost the sweaty bull hue it had previously acquired in Ian's apartment. Without waiting for Nata to finish speaking to him, Seba got up from his desk, snatched the paper from her hand and corroborated that he had indeed not misheard the victim's name. He then left her while she was midsentence and ran out to his vehicle.

First, no-clutch; second, no-clutch; accelerate, accelerate, third, brakes, second, yellow light, accelerate, no-clutch; third, accelerate, police, passing accident, horn, horn. As he drove to the municipal library, his mind kept thinking how on earth he had been able to do such a thing to Violeta without even knowing her.

At 10:16 a.m., Sebastián arrived at the library. At 10:17 a.m., Violeta was entering her house. Desperately, he tried calling her cell phone a dozen times but all his calls went straight to voicemail.

At 10:18 a.m., Sebastián was running out of the library. At 10:21 a.m., Violeta had finished placing the thirty-four candles throughout the house.

Without knowing it, both were exchanging actions minute by minute. Both had managed to choreograph their last encounter.

After placing all the candles in their specific positions, she began to light them. With each burning flame, she felt an intense odor escaping from them. They reeked of captive death, of a morbid putrefaction eager to spread. By the time she managed to finish lighting them all, the perfume in the house was unbearable, capable of penetrating and shattering the soul of any person. After several minutes of complete meditation, Violeta could not stand it any longer and tried to put an end to that stench of guilt, that reminder of guilt. So, she grabbed one of the candles with her right hand and walked towards the container that held the only fragrance capable of dampening that baleful stink. The exterior of the container was perfect for the occasion: painted red, with details in yellow and a flirtatious opening at the top that facilitated the spreading of its contents. Without hesitation, she sprayed the liquid in the bathroom, the four bedrooms, the kitchen, the small living room, the portraits she had with Sebastián and, finally, she bathed in its aroma. At 10:32 a.m., just as she was about to finish, Sebastián arrived.

"Violeta, Violeta, Violeta," Seba shouted from the steps of his house, "Are you there, Violeta, answer, are you there?"

"Go away, Sebastián. I love you, but I hate you and I can't live like this."

"No, I'm not leaving. You can't leave me like this, I have to explain, we have to talk; please, you have to listen to me; please forgive me. I didn't know anything. I was as incredulous as you. I know this sounds bad and it looks like I kept the details from you, but I swear I didn't know anything, the malpractice insurance companies keep me blind to the process so I don't do anything crazy. I swear I didn't know anything; I swear!"

Sebastián tried to open the door, but he couldn't, it was locked with a latch and deadbolted. He tried to look through the windows, designed to resist category five hurricanes, but he couldn't see clearly. Even if they had been open, it was humanly impossible to penetrate the steel bars protecting the entrance to the house. As he tried to make his way inside, his nose caught the smell of death that surrounded Violeta. With much more anxiety, he tried to make her react so that she would allow him to pass. Needless to say, he could not.

From inside the house, Violeta could only see a large debacle, surrounded by bonfires wrapped in glassy jars. The lights were out and the walls were bathed in orange light. For Violeta nothing made sense anymore. Her puritanical dignity had been shattered and thrown to the bottom of an impenetrable black abyss. In her mind there was only one sentence: "I am a whore who sold her mother for companionship and love." Even though it was not true, she kept repeating the same phrase to herself, until everything she saw seemed to come from far away. It was as if she were standing at the bottom of a well and her surroundings could only be perceived through a periscope.

As she wandered along the wet bottom of the well, she noticed that her feet were not immersed in water but in an intense, viscous and volatile perfume from the yellowish red bottle with which she had recently bathed. In addition, her hands, clothes, body and hair were all completely soaked in the liquid. There was not even a centimeter of her exempt from it. When Violeta looked at her body again, she noticed the lit candle was still in her right hand.

"I love you, Sebastián. I love you and I forgive you, but I can't forgive myself," Violeta shouted from inside her house.

"Violeta, I love you, don't do this. That criminal doctor who was guilty of the lawsuit is dead; I am no longer that man or doctor; please forgive me, don't do this," answered Seba, screaming from the bottom of his lungs.

As soon as these words reached her ears, Ms. Contreau dropped the glassed torch she held in her right hand to the bottom of that imaginary well. Although the candle's journey lasted only a second, for Violeta the moment lasted several minutes. At the bottom of the tunnel she was in, the image of her mother was projected until the glass framing the flames impacted the perfuming fragrance. Once the container was broken, the fire inside of it spread from her feet to the tips of her hair. In an instant, her body was burning to the rhythm of an organic liquid known as gasoline. Set ablaze, she watched as her house burned and the memories of her childhood disappeared with it. As she suffocated, wrapped in burning orange sheets, the elder daughter of Rocío Costas de Contreau was able to understand the enigmatic dream she once had in the Pérez-Fuertes family's lake house. She felt fear and indescribable pain as she died. As a result, she screamed and cried, letting out a shriek so terrifying that it seemed as if an infernal madness had taken over her last seconds of life. From the outside, even as her nerves screamed for help, her muscles remained paralyzed until her last breath.

"Violeta, get out of there, don't do it! Please don't do anything stupid, I'm dying without you! I love you, Violeta, I love you!" shouted Sebastián, banging on a door that was getting hotter by the minute as he kept trying to call the fire service from his cell phone.

Unfortunately, it was too late. Violeta was dead, burned, and her body was lying on the ground, charred by the flames.

Sebastián kept repeating between screams and tears, "I love you, come back, don't go, don't leave me, why did you do it?", until the firemen arrived and found him in front of the door of the house, beating it with his bloody and burned fists, coughing rabidly from smoke inhalation. A few hours later, they managed to put out the fire.

After Violeta's body was taken away and Sebastián was interrogated, they found a suicide letter signed by her inside the mailbox, which they did not let anyone see, but explained in a few words why she had set fire to her house and committed suicide, corroborating Seba's story.

As if he were a zombie, Dr. Pérez-Fuertes remained silent, standing in front of the remains of a completely ruined house. The ground was covered by a thick grayish paste composed of ash, water and smoke; nonetheless, he fell to his knees to say farewell. Slowly, Sebastián approached the mental image of where Violeta's tender smile, the one he loved so much, should have been. Blinded by his sadness and covered in smoke dust, mixed with tears, he leaned down and kissed her imaginary form, even though her charred body was already on its way to the morgue. For Seba, Violeta's illusory, ashen face dripped onto the floor like sand between his lips. To the firefighters, he was in a state of mental shock. That invisible kiss would be the last he would ever give in his life. Violeta was the last person who would ever touch his soul.

A few hours later that day, when after pulling his "doctor and fiancé card" he was allowed to see her in the morgue to identify her. Seba did not see her charred body, nor the grayish teeth (which were practically the only thing that remained of her). He only saw the tender image of a young woman, lying on the ground on that blissful day when he first saw her in front of his car. As he approached the corpse, one of the forensic pathologists asked him if he thought it was Violeta. Sebastián nodded his head and his gaze was so vacant that it appeared to be blind. The forensic pathology report confirmed Violeta Contreau as the burn victim, approximately two weeks after the fire, by matching dental records. For Sebastián, only two seconds were needed to identify her.

∬Final

With his clothes completely torn, his hands slightly burned and his lips covered with ashes, Seba drove from the morgue to the only place where he thought he could hide his pain. It had been raining for several hours. In fact, as he left Violeta's house, the first drops of a torrential downpour began to fall. It was as if the heavy torrent of rain was a function of the anguish and grief he carried within his soul.

When he arrived, he parked right in front of *El Bar del Murciégalo*. Although there were more people there than he would have liked, he only talked with *Hiswife* and *Hislover*. Sitting at the bar, the bartender, Antonio, served him twenty-two beers (12 fl. oz. each) during the almost nine hours he was there. Drunk as a skunk, he told the two rats in excruciating detail what had happened. At 9:53 p.m., after being imaginatively comforted by their company, Sebastián took his keys, which had turned into a loaded gun, and decided to drive away.

As he drove, the semi-automatic gears of his car didn't matter, nor the thirteen traffic lights he crossed without even looking, but which, luckily, were almost always green or yellow. Nor did the craters in the road matter, nor the raindrops that had been flooding Violeta's burned house for hours. For him, nothing in the world mattered anymore. Though highly irresponsible, Sebastián was not going to die behind the wheel that night; his time had not yet come.

When he arrived at the lake house, he opened the door and stumbled, wet from head to toe, to his bedroom. The level of alcohol in his blood was so high that he didn't notice anything that wasn't within a couple of feet of his sight. Lying on his bed, he turned on his television and used the "ANTENNA" button to recreate the memories of his morning. First, he watched Ian and the elf breaking into pieces, then he saw himself in front of Violeta's house trying to enter uselessly, finally, he relived the moment when he identified Violeta's body and her last goodbye kiss. Time after time, he rewound and watched every detail of his day until the clock struck 11:09 p.m. and he fell asleep.

Although neither Sebastián nor anyone else in the universe noticed, the lake surrounding the back of the mansion had received, since the burial of Don Samy, a punishing dose of heavy rains, which fell punctually and premeditatedly, increasing the water level like never before.

For this reason, the entire valley within the peninsula in which the Pérez family property was located was about to be submerged. Though Seba slept, he was unable to dream. His mind wandered in the void, as if waiting to be awakened.

It was exactly at 4:23 a.m. when all the letters received began to fulfill their prophecies. Sebastián woke up with a dry mouth and an unimaginable headache. Looking over at his desk, he discovered a note also written in black India ink. "Damn it," he thought, "damn Ian and his diabolical cult." The new note was, like the one from the day before, totally different from all the ones that had been received. This one had only one cipher:

365.25

Sebastián let go of it almost instantly and looked down at his TV, which was still on and began to emit a deafening screech that prompted him to turn it off. But try as he might, he could not. He tried to unplug it, to no avail. He tried to use the remote control, to no avail. So, he had to continue listening to it while the noise drilled his ears.

Suddenly, the annoying sound stopped and images began to appear on his screen. Undoubtedly, they showed the inside of Ian's apartment. "Am I still drunk?" he thought to himself, but his liver had already degraded all the alcohol that ran through his veins, he was completely sober. "Am I asleep?" he thought, as he rubbed his eyes, but the reality was that he had never been as awake as he was in those moments. He looked back up at the television and saw the image of his brother appear. In it, Ian was sitting similarly to the way Sebastián had left him when he departed his apartment. Although it did not say what time these images had happened, from the brightness of the day it could be inferred that it had been during the morning. Undeniably, what was happening had never been documented in his rules for using the "ANTENNA" button. Still, he decided to ignore this and concentrate on the images. Quietly, he watched his brother, Engr. Pérez-Fuertes remain in the same motionless pose without uttering a single word until, suddenly, his body came to life. Then he saw him get up, walk to the kitchen and open one of the cupboards under the sink. Since he couldn't see very well, Seba grabbed the remote control and enlarged the image. As he did so, he noticed how his brother was eating, in large quantities, something brownish-green that he could not identify. For several minutes he watched him eating until the bag was empty. Then Ian walked over to the pieces of what appeared to be a broken elf (Ernie) lying on the ground and fell on top of them.

Sebastián stiffened as the TV began to fast forward the images of his brother lying on the ground, as the window now showed the signs of the moon, sun, moon, moon, sun, moon, moon, sun, moon and sun, as if he was watching an accelerated image in the future of what would happen inside Ian's apartment. Suddenly, the TV went back to showing the actions in real time. Sebastián felt an absolute chill run through his bones as, looking at his brother's face, he saw streams of blood begin to spurt from his mouth. However, he became paralyzed when he saw him convulsing, falling face up, while the blood not only spurted from his lips, but also from his ears, nose and eyes, creating a huge hemorrhage that would soon end his life. As soon as he realized what was happening to him, he knew what his brother had so eagerly eaten in the kitchen. Ian had taken his own life by ingesting, *bromadiolone,* rat poison, which he had recently purchased to kill the rodent infestation in his apartment. His veins were more anticoagulated than a syringe of heparin. Unfortunately, there was not a single useful molecule of vitamin K in his body.

"Nooooo!" cried Sebastián disconsolately.

Instinctively, he grabbed the television set and smashed it against a huge mirror hanging in his bedroom. To his surprise, neither the mirror nor the TV broke. In fact, the latter bounced and fell on the floor, disconnected from the electricity, showing the agonizing final moments of his brother's life. Watching as he convulsed, he knew with certainty that he would die very soon, either from a lethal heart rhythm or a myocardial infarction (i.e., a heart attack) or, most likely, from the massive brain bleed that had caused his seizures. Ironically, Ian would die the same way Violeta's mother died, from a massive hemorrhage.

Navigating the agony of having just seen his brother die and only hours after having identified his fiancée, Violeta, as the burn victim in the morgue, Sebastián was startled by a rhythmic echo that seemed to be the sound of a rush of water coming from the windows. Indeed, when he turned around, he discovered that the landscape in the distance no longer showed an ounce of air, but a watery fluid with a dark, brown and red appearance, almost like the color of a bloody mud that was trying to enter his bedroom. In fact, the outside of the house was completely submerged by the lake and the inside would certainly be the next destination of its stream within the next few minutes. "Can it be true or am I imagining it?" he thought, as he saw flashes of light in his room that would later give way to the appearance of replicas of the final note.

Progressively, these flashes of light took over every nook and cranny of his bedroom until the digits "365.25, 365.25, 365.25…" became thousands of lines that completely covered his room. Even though Sebastián knew what it meant, it still hadn't dawned on him why his days were up, if he still had just under a week to live, perhaps between six to seven days, by his calculations. In essence, Sebastián's mistake was that his count of consecutive letters was not accurate, since his last year of life, or his 365.25 elapsed days, did not start from the day he met Violeta, as he believed, but from the week before, when he visited France from his apartment, as a result of the first lethal note.

However, Sebastián would not die ignorant of this fact. On that immense mirror in his bedroom began to be projected the images, from the newest to the oldest, of the notes received along with the count of days and hours at which they were delivered. Projected on the mirror, he watched each of the anonymously delivered notes pass by at an accelerated pace, until he observed how the seventh one skipped all the way to the first. It was then that he realized that his calculations were wrong and that all the warnings could be accurate. Then, Sebastián stood still for several moments, while he looked at the last note (in essence, the first one) and its validation data. For a moment, he recognized the handwriting and calligraphy on them. "How strange, I recognize that penmanship. Could I be the author? Have I written these notes while asleep or while under some other deranged personality?" he thought, as he felt the rest of the universe collapse inside his soul. Inwardly, he tried to convince himself that it wasn't him who caused all that anguish, but in the end, he became so disillusioned and empty that he decided to accept the blame, without even remembering it. "Am I completely possessed by a multiple personality disorder? Am I bipolar or schizophrenic? How could I unblock from my present having written so many letters?" he wondered. And, as he looked at his hands, he realized that they were completely covered in black India ink. For all intents and purposes, those black ink marks on his fingers were as compromising as if they were covered in blood and holding a gigantic knife next to a recently stabbed person. The only problem was that, now, the victim and the victimizer were the same. Apparently, Sebastián had been stabbing his feelings for a whole year, without even suspecting it.

Completely evicted by his spirit, surrounded by the hundreds of thousands of lines that read "365.25, 365.25, 365.25..." he began to experience a kind of electromagnetic force that attracted him to his image in the mirror. As a result, he walked to his reflection and the more he looked at his image, the more drawn he was to it. Suddenly, he felt as if his world was being exchanged. Everything around him distorted and changed perspective, creating a dramatic oscillation between his perception and that of his surroundings. For several seconds he felt dizzy and disoriented, but as soon as he was able to focus his vision he was in control of his state.

Undoubtedly, Sebastián had changed bodies. Now he was no longer the one standing in front of the mirror, but had become the reflection of the one who was looking at him. Without knowing how, he found himself inside the mirror and it was strange because, although he knew that he was still himself, he was not really who he once was. With great determination he began to simultaneously hit the mirror from both sides of the reflective sheet, but it was useless, he could never break it, he was trapped.

"Am I dead?" he wondered, "Am I still alive?"

As he tried to answer himself, the strong beating of his heart prevented him from doing so. In fact, his chest was not pounding for fear of dying in the early hours of that morning. In his opinion, he was already more dead than alive; his brother and his fiancée had committed suicide, his father had passed away from terminal lung cancer only a couple of weeks ago while he was trying to save him, failing as a doctor, and his mother, though physically alive, was essentially dead. As always happens when someone is in a deep depression, he did not think of Natalia or Doña Mama, both of whom were still worth fighting for or that he could try to rebuild his life with their help. Nor did he think of his profession, of saving patients as a doctor, traveling the world on missions to poorer countries in need. Finally, it didn't even occur to him to seek psychiatric help so that he wouldn't have to throw it all away. No, he simply felt totally alone, hopeless. For him, the poetic meaning of life had been extinguished. Despite this, and without knowing why, he felt afraid. He feared remaining alive and being imprisoned inside that cold, crystalline wall. He felt horror of not being able to escape and, as a consequence, being condemned to a life sentence of solitude.

Then his focus changed and he began to panic as he worried that the premonitory notes could be perhaps not true, that he was not their author, even though everything pointed to the fact that he was, that he would forever have to bear the pain of the loss of his family and Violeta. After thinking about this, his anxiety increased and he began to feel short of breath. He then watched as his counterpart image slowly walked backwards and fell into the bed, lying motionless, staring up at the ceiling. For several minutes, the Sebastián trapped inside the mirror watched himself paralyzed, stiff, and knew that any sign of sanity had been drained from that almost inert body. Seeing his partially catatonic image, lying in front of himself, he realized that he was no longer even the same reflection of his other self. Somehow, both beings were two different souls and bodies.

"And who am I?" he asked himself, "and who is he?"

Quickly, he reflected on his mental state with a crystalline, almost surgical clarity. He thought about the premonitory notes he might have written under some other multiple personality and his use of the "ANTENNA" button, which were but thousands of recorded hallucinations of his life. He deliberated on his family and on his genetic predisposition to mental illness, including clinical diagnoses learned in his psychiatry and psychology classes. Then he looked at his reflection on the bed, almost paralyzed, and knew that whoever he was looking at from afar would never be part of himself.

Hoping to escape forever from that captivity, he began to contemplate the idea of drowning in Lake *La Plata*. Because of this, he desperately looked at the floor to see if water was already seeping into his bedroom through the windows. When he did so, he realized that there was not a single drop on the tiles. The floor was completely dry. For several moments he lost all hope that his anguish would end until suddenly, he began to see some reddish-orange drops falling from the ceiling. He looked up and, as he did so, realized that the liquid was not pooling on the ground to rise but, defying the laws of gravity, had collected on the ceiling and was now embedded high above, intending to drown them as it descended.

Suddenly, he began to see something strange moving on the mirror, right in front of his eyes. After several seconds he deciphered what it was he saw. It was letters, from his point of view reversed, that were beginning to darken in black ink. With the appearance of the letters, he also began to observe that both his bedroom and his "un-captive-unhinged-and-catatonic self" faded away and were replaced by a blurred image of a totally unknown person. The person seemed to have the same need as he did to find out what was written on those lines. It was as if both he and his new reading companion were carefully studying a book face to face, separated by their reflections. Even though the letters appeared in reverse, written on the other side of the mirror, Sebastián was able to read them. Hopeful now that it might be true, that he would indeed die that night, he looked up to the top of the ceiling and watched as the water continued to descend. His eyes moved up and down, right and left, chasing his and his new companion's reading, giving a cathartic touch with its passage, purifying every feeling contained within Sebastián's soul and cleansing the contents of every past event lived, including his present and the future they were both about to read.

Then, and only then, for the first time in a year, did he rejoice at the hundreds of premonitory letters received, no matter who the author was. For Sebastián it no longer mattered if it had been God, the Devil, a fictitious unbelievable cult, or himself by means of another personality (who was now lying on his bed, with black India ink marks on his hands, acting like a totally deranged man). He really didn't care who created them anymore. That early morning would, in one way or another, be some version of the end of his life. Faithfully, every drop of water that covered the letters reaffirmed his potential to drown. As a result, he decided to lean back against the bottom of the mirror, as close as he could to the floor, with the intention of finishing the last paragraph they were both reading.

In that moment, lying in a fetal position, Sebastián witnessed the final omen of the end of his life. Slowly, while he and his reading companion digested those final written lines, each solitary letter and word drew closer and closer to his body. Meticulously, that alphabet of liquid symbols was slipping into his nose and passing through his pharynx, until he was forced to inhale deeply with his mouth to keep breathing, trying unsuccessfully to prevent his lungs from prematurely suffocating. Finally, in the last seconds of his existence, he tried to fantasize about Violeta, growing old by her side, sitting every night in front of the same lake that in this precise moment seemed hell-bent on taking his life. Unfortunately, both the lack of oxygen and the excess of carbon dioxide briefly brought him back to his solitary reality. Consequently, he had to try to concentrate a little more in order to finish, in full, all the words written in front of the mirror. Thankfully, he was able to imagine himself once again back together with the love of his life, eternally happy and enamored. In that instant, he found absolute peace and had the extreme certainty that at the end of that last written sentence, in the presence of that companion who was reading next to him, both his present life and that of the previous Dr. Sebastián Luis Pérez-Fuertes would forever cease to exist.